Only One

for Me

CANDACE SHAW

Only One for Me

Candace Shaw

Copyright © 2013 by Candace Shaw

All Rights Reserved.

Copyright by Candace Shaw, June 2013

Cover Art by Shaw Press, June 2013

Edited by Melissa M. Ringsted

ISBN **978-1490476377**

Shaw Press

Atlanta, Georgia

ACKNOWLEDGEMENTS

A special thank you to readers, Sherika Williams and Ollie Moss who won the opportunity for me to create two characters by using their names. Thank you so much, ladies!

PART ONE

CHAPTER ONE

14 years ago...

Cannon Arrington raced along the interstate in his white Mustang, shifting gears and weaving in and out of traffic. He'd overslept, as usual, and was running late to the Read-a-Thon at Garrett A. Morgan Elementary School. A second-year medical student at Meharry Medical College, he'd stayed up until three in the morning working on a presentation he had to give at noon. He'd hit the snooze button on the alarm clock a few times before realizing he had overslept.

Glancing at the time on the dash, he had twenty minutes to be seated in a first grade teacher's rocking chair to read a book. He'd volunteered with the graduate chapter of his fraternity, which adopted the school as a partner in education in order to show a more visible presence of positive African-American men as role models. His best friend and fraternity brother, Doug Winters, presided over the program and had persuaded Cannon to participate, which only added more to his already overflowing plate of activities outside of medical school.

He pulled into a parking space, popped the trunk, and grabbed the crate of books before he dashed into the front door of the school. Since it was the beginning of October, he decided he would read *Stellaluna* by Janell Cannon. It was one of his favorite books about a fruit bat that was raised by birds. He'd brought enough copies for each student in the class to have.

"What up, frat?"

Cannon turned his attention to the left to find Doug, who was dressed in a pair of khaki's, a black polo shirt with their fraternity crest, and holding a clipboard. Cannon had on the same attire. They met each other halfway.

"Good morning, Doug. Great minds think alike." They shook hands while doing their secret handshake, which went unnoticed by people walking by.

"Yes, except when it comes to setting the alarm clock. I had to switch you and Tony. You're now reading in Ms. Dubose's classroom. I'll walk with you."

"Dubose? My favorite teacher from high school was Ms. Dubose."

"Well, I doubt it's her. She's Sherika's best friend. They're from Memphis, like you, and teach across the hall from each other."

Cannon glanced sideways at his friend. "Oh, so that's why you chose this school," he said with a smirk. "Because your new girlfriend teaches here."

"She's not my girlfriend." They turned down a bright yellow hallway with colorful bulletin boards displaying student's work. "We're just hanging and getting to know each other." The gentlemen stopped in front of a door displaying cut-out autumn leaves falling from a tree. "Here's Ms. Dubose's classroom. I'll be across the hall reading," Doug said with a grin and a wink.

Cannon chuckled. "I'm sure you will be."

He turned toward the classroom door, shifted the crate of books on his left hip, and pushed open the already ajar door.

Approximately twenty students sat on an oversized carpet of the United States in front of a bulletin board with a calendar, student work, and a dry erase board. The students were listening intently as their teacher sat in a rocking chair, reading a book to them in the sweetest voice he'd ever heard.

"Ms. Dubose, we have company," a little boy stated in a loud tone.

She lifted her head, wearing a breathtaking smile on her angelic face, and his heart skipped a few beats. Her smile grew even wider and even more amazing as she tilted her head to the left with a look of recognition on her face. She handed the book to a little girl sitting in front of her. The teacher stood and proceeded toward him at the back of the classroom while the little girl continued reading the book to the class. He watched as the young teacher moved gracefully in a pair of gray dress slacks and a black, short-sleeved sweater, which complimented her small frame. Her sandy brown, layered bob framed her soft face, but he couldn't take his eyes off her smile. It warmed his heart.

She stopped a few feet in front of him and held out her hand. He set the crate of books on a desk and took her small hand into his.

"Hello. I'm Ms. Dubose. Welcome to my classroom."

"Thank you, Ms. Dubose. I'm Cannon Arrington."

She glanced at the students, who were sitting nicely on the carpet while their classmate read to them. "You probably don't remember me, but my mother is Emma Dubose at Frederick Douglass High in Memphis."

"She was my favorite teacher, and I do remember you." He paused and lowered his voice so the students wouldn't hear. "*Yasmine*. You would do your homework after school in your mother's classroom during our science club meetings. Surprised to see you in Nashville."

Yasmine flashed her beautiful smile again, and he had to hold in a sigh. She was so breathtaking. She had definitely grown up from the geeky, little freshman he remembered sitting shyly in her mother's classroom with her nose in a book. She was all woman now, and a fine one at that.

"I attended TSU. I just graduated in May and was offered a job here. And you?"

"I'm a student over at Meharry."

"Cool. Small world." She looked in the direction of her students as the little girl finished reading. The children had begun to speak quietly. "I'm so surprised to see you. I thought someone else was coming to read."

"Doug switched us. Well, I guess I better go read." He grabbed his autographed copy of *Stellaluna* and followed her toward the front of the classroom. He tried to keep his eyes straight ahead; however, they kept glancing at the cutest butt he'd ever seen.

The children's voices silenced when they saw their teacher approach. She stood next to the rocking chair and displayed that damn smile again. Cannon cleared his throat and tried to stay focused. He was there to read not lust over the teacher, but if she kept flashing that smile and shining her pretty brown, doe-like eyes on him, he wouldn't be able to concentrate.

"All right class. Let's welcome Mr. Arrington, a student at Meharry Medical College." Yasmine motioned for him to sit in her rocking chair. "What do we say, boys and girls?"

"Good morning, Mr. Arrington," all of the students said at once.

"Good morning, students," he said in an upbeat tone as he sat down. He glanced at Yasmine, who gave him an encouraging nod. She walked to her desk and perched on top of it. The sexy, bubbly teacher with the simply amazing smile was doing a number on him. He cleared his throat, opened the book, and prayed he could keep focused on reading and not Yasmine.

Yasmine stared at Cannon as he read one of her favorite books to her class. She couldn't believe when she looked up and saw Cannon Arrington, her high school crush, standing in the back of her classroom. She'd almost fallen out of her rocking chair, but instead, quickly handed the book she was reading to one of her brightest students.

Of course, he never really spoke to her in high school; just an occasional hello or nod if he saw her in the hallway, but only because her mother was his mentor. He probably did so out of obligation considering he was a senior, and she was only a freshman. A nerdy, gawky-looking freshman with braces and whose mother was a science teacher at the school. Boys didn't even notice her until her junior year, when she somewhat blossomed, but were scared to ask her out because of her mother.

When she was fourteen, she thought he was the most handsome boy she'd ever laid her eyes on. Now at twenty-two, he was the most handsome man she'd ever seen. Her gaze casually roamed his chiseled face with the strong jaw line, butterscotch kissed skin and low-cut wavy hair. His deep, baritone voice—that sounded like a baby bird at the moment—sent electric shocks through every cell in her body. His over-powering presence seemed to take over the classroom. Around six feet one with a medium-build frame, he was way too big for her rocking chair.

She grabbed her camera to take a few pictures of Cannon and her students for the Read-a-Thon bulletin board and for her personal photo album, of course. She was disappointed when Cannon was done with his question and answer period. When she saw him glance at his watch, making a slight grimace, she knew it was time to wrap up.

"Thank you, boys and girls. I brought each of you a copy of *Stellaluna.*

The students cheered and clapped. Yasmine slipped from her desk and walked over to stand next to the rocking chair. His masculine, woodsy scent tantalized her nostrils, causing her to go weak for a second, but she quickly shifted gears and put on her teacher's hat.

"What do we say, class?"

"Thank you, Mr. Arrington," the students exclaimed in unison.

"You're very welcome. It was my pleasure." Cannon stood, and Yasmine's heart sunk a little. He was leaving.

"Can you come back next Friday?" a little boy asked, and the rest of the class began to beg in their cute little six-year old voices. Yasmine silently begged in her head. *Pretty please? With a cherry on top?*

Cannon smiled sincerely at them. "I'll set something up with your teacher, but it may not be next Friday."

After the students gave him a group hug and high-fives, Cannon waited by the door while Yasmine dismissed the students to their desks and instructed them to begin working on the grammar questions on the board. She pressed play on the CD player and the sounds of Mozart filled the room. Once they were settled, she met Cannon at the back of the classroom.

"Thank you so much for reading to my class today. You did very well with them."

"Thank you. I'm going to be a pediatrician one day, so I hope children will like me. I meant what I said about coming back. I'm always available to give a helping hand." He reached into his wallet and handed her a card with his phone number and email address. "Just call me."

His voice was smooth and casual with a hint of seduction, which flustered her to no end. She ran her hand through her hair and hoped when she spoke her tongue wouldn't be tied in knots. "Thank ... you," she stammered. "The fall festival is coming up, and I'm sure the PTA will need extra help."

"Whatever you need," he said with a sexy half grin. "Well ... I hate to read and run, but I have a study group meeting in an hour. Plus, I have to go back home to pick up my sister, Raven, whose car is acting up. She's also in her second year at Meharry."

"I remember your twin sister. Wow, you're both in medical school? Your parents must be very proud."

He chuckled, displaying his gorgeous smile and a cute dimple on his left cheek. "They are, but they're both doctors. They've been training us since birth to be doctors as well. My brother, Sean, is at Morehouse and should be coming to Meharry in a few years if he can keep his mind on his books and not on the girls at Spelman."

Yasmine laughed, even though deep down she was disappointed he had to leave.

"Well, I gotta go." He stepped toward her, as if he was about to hug her, but then glanced at the students. Instead, they shook hands and a spark of static electricity shocked them both. Her temperature rose, and she had a feeling her cheeks were flushed pink, as they always were when she was embarrassed.

He winked and a charismatic grin flashed across his handsome face.

"It was really, *really* good to see you again, Yasmine," he said in a low, deep voice and squeezed her hand with a tender caress before letting it go.

After he left, she tried to put her focus on her class for the rest of the morning, but her thoughts kept racing back to Cannon.

Even though it had been almost eight years since she'd seen him, he still had the same captivating intellect and sexy charm that had attracted her to him in the first place. But now he was a grown man. Now she wanted him more than ever.

CHAPTER TWO

"Girl, guess what?" Yasmine squealed as she sat down with her lunch at the group center table to join her best friend, and first-grade teacher, Sherika Williams. As first year teachers, they opted to eat their lunch in the classroom instead of the teacher's lounge to avoid all of the gossip.

Sherika finished chewing her homemade lasagna and a wicked smile crossed her face. "Did you hear some more rumors about the principal and Ms. Woods? Spill the tea!"

"No, better. Cannon Arrington read to my class this morning."

"Really?" She paused, with her fork almost to her lips. "You didn't faint did you?"

"Almost. He's even dreamier than he was in high school. I was so nervous."

"Did he remember you?"

"Yes, but only after I mentioned my mother."

"Well ... "

"Well, what?" Yasmine asked before taking a bite of her chicken salad sandwich.

"Are you going to stay in contact with him?" She pushed her shoulder length hair behind her ear to avoid marina sauce on it.

"He gave me his phone number if I want him to volunteer or something, but he didn't ask for mine." She shrugged. "So ... I don't I know. Probably not."

"Why is he in Nashville?"

"Medical school. I guess he knows your man since they're fraternity brothers."

"Doug is not my man. Besides, he accepted the job offer in New York. He starts in two weeks." Sherika shrugged it off, but Yasmine could tell her friend was disappointed.

"Well, maybe you can date long-distance."

"Naw ... it wasn't serious. But we agreed to stay in contact, which means we won't." Sherika pushed her food around with her fork. "Plus, he was so wishy-washy sometimes, and I don't have time for that."

"Well, at least you've had someone to date. I haven't had a decent date since ... who knows," Yasmine said, with a delicate lift of her shoulder.

"You went out with that guy a few weeks ago."

"I said a *decent* date. He talked about himself the entire time and was rude to the waitress."

Buzz.

The timer sounded on Yasmine's desk, letting them know that they had five more minutes before it was time to pick up their classes from the cafeteria.

"Lunch goes by so fast," Sherika said. "At least it's Friday. What are you doing for the rest of the afternoon?" She stood and grabbed her blue suit jacket from the chair, placing her container back into her small cooler.

"Thank you cards after their math test. Cannon gave each student a copy of the book he read, and since we've been discussing how to write a friendly letter this past week, it will be another way for the students to practice."

"Neat. I'm stealing your idea. See you later."

During the afternoon, Yasmine's class worked on their thank you cards and drew pictures of scenes from the book. She tried to stay focused, but nerves overtook her as she thought about whether or not to contact Cannon to give him the cards. She'd promised her students she would make sure he received them, and if he ever came to visit again, she knew that would be the first question they would ask.

That evening, Yasmine sat on the couch with her laptop and all of the thank you cards stacked up on the coffee table. She decided she was going to email Cannon and ask him for his address so she could mail the cards in one big envelope, along with the pictures of him reading to the students.

Muffled hip-hop music began to reverberate through the ceiling, quickly followed by a loud crash interrupting her contemplative mood. She sighed and stared up in the apartment she'd lived in since her senior year of college. Apparently, the new tenants above her were having a party, as usual. At the time, it made sense to rent an apartment a few miles from campus, but now she was ready to move.

Trying to tune the music out, she read over the email, deleted it for the fifth time, and began to type out another one.

"Dear Cannon ... no wait ... that's too formal." She deleted it. "Hey, Cannon. No wait. *Hey* is for a horse, at least that's what my mother says. Let's see. Hi, Cannon. Yep. That's better."

Hi, Cannon!

Thank you so much for reading to my class today. My students enjoyed it very much. To show their appreciation, they made you thank you cards, and I would like to mail them to you. If you could send me your address when you have a chance that would be great, or call me at 555-0819.

Sincerely,

Yasmine Dubose
"Perfect. That sounds better."

She read it ten times, deleted it, walked away from the computer, typed it again, deleted it, took a shower, retyped it without her phone number, and then added it back in.

Okay, this is ridiculous. You aren't the shy little girl you were in high school. It shouldn't take two hours to send an email. You're a strong, independent woman who simply needs a handsome man's address to honor the request of her students.

Yasmine pressed send and closed her laptop before she changed her mind.

Chime.

Cannon glanced at his laptop when his email account notified him he had a new message. He was reading over a ten page paper he received back that afternoon and wasn't interested in anything outside of it.

Sheesh.

He received a B+ because he had a few typos. He hated anything less than an A, unless it was a hard B, but he was too intelligent and too much of a perfectionist to even accept that. The professor had written a note in red on the cover page:

Excellent A paper, but you need to get a proofreader for the next one because I may not be so lenient next time.

Cannon read through the paper, taking note of all of his careless mistakes. He was surprised at his errors, but Raven blamed it on his lack of sleep and taking on too many outside projects. She was the more focused twin who concentrated only on her classes and elected not to have any extracurricular activities outside of medical school.

Chime.

Cannon tossed the paper on his desk and proceeded to his bed, where the laptop sat. He had two emails waiting. One was from his sister, Bria, and one from Yasmine Dubose. Baby sister could wait. He clicked on Yasmine's name and read the short message, imagining her bubbly voice in his head.

He read it again and smiled. He'd been thinking about her off and on during the day and kicking himself for not getting her phone number, but he thought it would be inappropriate to ask for it in her classroom. Instead, he'd planned on asking Doug to set something up with Sherika and Yasmine to see her again, but now he didn't have to. Her number was staring back at him on the screen.

He quickly checked his sister's email. At seventeen, Bria was into boys, shopping, and sports. Captain of her soccer team, she wanted him to know that they'd won the game thanks to her winning kick and that their youngest sibling, Shelbi, had been elected to sophomore class president. He emailed Bria back with congratulations to both sisters.

His stomach grumbled, reminding him of something he'd meant to do since two o'clock. Eat. He glanced at his watch. It was nine at night.

He proceeded to the kitchen as he dialed Yasmine's number and opened the refrigerator. The left over pizza was gone. *Thanks, Raven.* Everything else was breakfast food. He grabbed the eggs, cheese, an onion, a bell pepper, and ham to make an omelet.

"Hello?"

His heart smiled at the sound of her beautiful voice in his ear.

"Hi, Yasmine. This is Cannon Arrington. Are you busy?"

"Nope. Just grading papers."

"Working on a Friday night? I'm surprised a woman as adorable as you isn't out on a date."

"Thanks for the compliment, but I needed a break. The last few dates I've been on were horrible. One guy just rambled on about himself the entire time."

"He was probably nervous being around you. Some men become big blabbermouths when in the presence of a lovely woman."

She giggled. "Thank you."

"Just speaking the truth."

Silence.

He cleared his throat. "So how's your mother?"

"She's fine. Still teaching AP biology and chemistry. She only has a few more years before retirement, but I have a feeling she'll work beyond that."

"Your mother is a wonderful teacher. I learned so much from her."

"Thank you. I'll let her know you asked about her. I wanted to get your address so I can send you the thank you cards."

"Of course." He whisked the eggs into a bowl. "Let me know when you're ready to jot it down."

After he gave her his address, they caught up on their lives since high school, her funny stories about teaching so far, and her noisy neighbors. He let her do most of the talking because he wanted to know everything about her; plus, he enjoyed listening to her bubbly, sweet voice. She wasn't the nerdy, shy teenager he remembered. She was full of life and had blossomed into a delightful, intelligent woman.

Before he realized it, it was after two o'clock in the morning. He'd retreated to his bedroom after eating his omelet and had stretched out on top of the comforter.

"Yasmine, I didn't realize what time it was…" His sentence trailed off into a yawn. "It's 2:15 in the morning."

She yawned. "Yeah … it sure is," she replied in a sleepy tone and yawned again. "Cannon, stop yawning. You're making me yawn. I have to be up at six in the morning for a breast cancer walk."

"I'll let you go to bed."

"I'm already in bed," she moaned. "Nice and snug."

Her moan wasn't supposed to be sexual, but the thought of her *nice and snug* in bed had his mind in the gutter. It was definitely time to let her go, even though he didn't want to. Instead, he'd rather listen to her sleepy moans in his ear until the sun came up.

"It was really nice talking with you."

Silence.

"Yasmine?"

"Huh … mmmm … Cannon?"

I see a cold shower in my future if she keeps moaning and saying my name like that.

"I'm going to let you go to sleep now," he said reluctantly. "Have fun at the walk."

"Mmmm … okay. You too."

He chuckled. She was definitely drifting off to sleep. "Go ahead and hang up."

"Good night, Cannon." Her voice was barely above a whisper, and he loved the way she said his name as if she'd been saying it for years. As if she was the only woman meant to say it like that. It stirred in him a fervor that he couldn't explain.

"Sweet dreams, Yasmine."

CHAPTER THREE

The ringing of her phone interrupted Yasmine's peaceful moment in a warm bubble bath to relax her muscles. Even though she worked out all of the time, her body was sore from walking and jogging five miles that morning at the breast cancer walk. She reached for the phone on the side of the tub and glanced at the name on the screen. "C. Arrington."

"Oh my goodness it's him!" In her excitement, the cordless phone slipped from her fingers and into the tub of bubbles. She fished around for it, but the phone had drowned, even though she could hear the other cordless ringing from her adjoining bedroom. She stepped out of the tub, grabbed the towel from the bar, and ran soaking wet to the still ringing phone. She knew it would stop soon. She'd set it to ring twelve times before going to voicemail.

"Hello?" she said in cheery, breathless voice.

"Hey. It's Cannon."

She knew he'd spoken, but because she was in such shock that he'd called her, she wasn't sure what he'd said, and it took her a moment to process it. Yasmine never thought she was the type of woman to be flustered over a man and not able to control herself, but Cannon Arrington was causing her imagination to run rampant.

"Hi. How are you?" she finally managed to say.

"I'm doing great. How was the breast cancer walk?"

"It went really well. I was sleepy most of the day because somebody kept me up all night." She finished drying off and laid across the bed.

"I've been known to do that before and no one has ever complained," he said in a sexy, cocky tone.

Heated sensations flowed through her body from his unexpected flirtatious answer. She cleared her throat. "How was your day?"

"Busy, as usual. Frat meeting this morning, study group this afternoon, and now I'm taking a break from writing a paper that's due in a few weeks. Plus, I need to fill out a grant application for a medical study I hope to do the summer after I graduate."

"You're a busy guy. Do you ever relax? Take a break?" She turned over on her back and stared up at the ceiling fan. She thought about her father, who had been a workaholic. He never stopped to smell the roses and died from his second heart attack when Yasmine was ten.

"My head isn't always in a book. I go out to clubs or listen to live music when I have a chance. So … when can I see you again? Maybe you can help me relax."

Her heart stopped, and there was a quiver in the pit of her stomach. Was he asking her out on a date? "Well … I don't know. When will you have some free time?"

"Tonight, if you're available."

"Tonight?" She sat all the way up and looked at her clock. It was six on the dot.

"Yes. While I do enjoy hearing your voice in my ear, I'd much rather see your adorable face."

Her heart thumped so loud in her chest, she was sure he could hear it through the phone. "Okay, and I can bring the thank you cards since I haven't mailed them yet."

"Bring them along with your sweet smile and cute little giggle."

She giggled.

"Yep, that's the one."

His voice was deep and seductive, and it was making her hot.

"Are you flirting with me?" Not that she minded.

"Yes, and it must be working since you've agreed to go on a date with me."

"Date? I just need to give you the cards my students made for you," she teased.

"It's a date because I said it's a date."

"Okay, then I guess it is." It took everything she had not to jump up and down on her bed, but she remained calm. *I'll call Sherika and squeal in her ear.* "Have you eaten dinner yet? There's this new hot spot not far from downtown that has the best barbeque and live music on Saturday nights. Reminds me of Beale Street in Memphis."

"Sounds good to me."

"Cool. I can meet you there." She rushed to the closet to see what on earth she was going to wear. It was the beginning of October, therefore it was cooler at night, but she wanted to wear something flirty and sexy that showed off her toned legs.

"I don't mind picking you up," he said casually.

She stopped tossing dresses onto her bed. She'd established dating rules when she moved off campus and into her apartment. One of the rules was: Don't let a man know where you live until after the third date.

But this was Cannon Arrington. It wasn't as if she didn't know him. He was a nice guy, he was in medical school, and her mother liked him.

"All right," she said walking toward the bathroom. "Is eight okay?

"Absolutely."

At exactly eight 'o' clock, Cannon rang Yasmine's doorbell. A few seconds later, he was graced with her breathtaking presence and a face so beautiful it could launch a thousand ships.

"Hi," she said with a smile.

"Wow," he sighed. "You look simply amazing." He perused her short, colorful sundress stopping just above her knees. The dress showed off her feminine curves and enhanced her caramel-coated smooth skin—especially her toned legs. He tried to shake off the image of her legs being wrapped around his waist, as he continued his journey down to hot pink, wedged sandals where her dainty toes with coral-colored toenails peeked out. His eyes settled back on her face, which was flushed after the exploration he gave her body. He couldn't help it; the woman was beautiful inside and out.

Thirty minutes later they were seated at the restaurant and looking over their menus. Well, she was looking at hers. Cannon was focused on her, as were the other males in the restaurant; from the waiters, customers, busboys, and even the musicians in the band setting up their equipment. They were all stealing glances just like him. Who could blame them? Yasmine had the type of natural beauty that didn't require long hours in the mirror. Cannon felt his male ego get bigger. She was *his* date for the evening.

"This is a really nice restaurant," he said, closing his menu after deciding what he would order. "I'd heard about it, but haven't had a chance to check it out. I'm always on the go."

"You need to get out and relax sometimes. Enjoy life."

"I know, but a brother's got things to do," he jokingly replied.

She laughed, sharing her smile again with him.

"So, are you ready for Christmas vacation?" he asked after the waiter took their order.

"I'm definitely looking forward to those two weeks off."

"I bet. Are you going home to Memphis to visit your mother?"

"No, my mom and her two best friends from Atlanta are going on a girl's cruise during that time."

"What are you going to do for Christmas?" he questioned, his voice filled with concern.

"My mother and I stopped celebrating it after my father died on Christmas Eve when I was ten. Christmas hasn't felt the same since." She shrugged her shoulders. A wistful expression loomed over her face, and Cannon reached over to caress her hand. She gave a weak smile.

"I had no idea." He squeezed her hand.

"He had a heart attack. It was his second one. My father didn't know how to slow down and just relax. He loved his career as a financial analyst. He was always busy, never home ... when he was home, he was locked in his office on the phone discussing business."

They were interrupted by the waiter bringing their appetizer of spinach dip with pita bread.

"You don't want to go with your mother on the cruise?" he asked after they began to eat.

"No. It's for people her age. You know, the grown and sexy crowd. Some of her teacher friends who are divorced or widowed as well are going. I'll be fine. I'm thinking about finding a holiday job, like wrapping gifts at a department store. I'm saving for a house."

"Have you started looking at houses?"

"No, but I want to begin saving so I can have a down payment and money left over to decorate it. I'm paying rent for an apartment when I could pay slightly more for a mortgage and actually own my own home."

"I'm impressed. That's a very good investment. My sister and I live in the house my parents bought when they got married and began their residencies after graduating from Meharry. They decided to keep it as rental property when they moved back to Memphis, and I'm grateful that they did."

The DJ turned off the music and announced the blues band. Yasmine and Cannon halted their conversation as they ate dinner and listened to the band play, while glancing and smiling at each other the entire time.

Cannon's eyes couldn't stray from her. Stealing glances at her side profile, since she turned to see the band, he felt his breathing waver before starting again. His gaze inched down to where he could see her small, yet perky, breasts outlined on her dress. He wasn't a man concerned with the size of a woman's breasts. They were all kissable, lickable, nibbleable and delicious. His manhood tightened at the thought of tasting hers and anywhere else she wanted him to. He straightened in his chair as she placed her eyes on him and smiled with her succulent lips before turning her attention back on the band.

Those damn mouthwatering lips of hers were downright sexy. They were painted with a light shade of pink which shimmered on her tempting pouty mouth, forcing his gaze to linger there. There was something about her lips encasing her smile which sent ripples of need shooting through to his groin. He cleared his throat and tried to focus on the blues band, but it took all of his strength not to reach out and pull her on his lap and shower her with kisses.

"Well, I had a really nice time," Yasmine said as Cannon pulled into her apartment complex and parked. She was contemplating whether or not to invite him in to watch a movie. She didn't want the night to end.

"Me, too." He turned off the ignition but didn't move. Instead, he drew in a long breath and exhaled slowly. His stare was intense, and the knot in her stomach tightened.

She could feel her pulse race through her veins as she stared straight ahead to avoid his hot gaze, which she could feel more than she could see. She reached for the door handle, but felt a warm hand on her left one. She turned to look at Cannon as he raised her hand to his lips and kissed it softly. Her body quivered at his touch, and the urge to kiss him burned on her lips. His free hand caressed her cheek and he pulled her chin closer to him as he leaned in and kissed her lips, as a breathless moan erupted from her throat.

The tender touch of his lips on hers stimulated a pool of heat to elicit from her center. His kiss deepened with every second that passed, sinking her more into an oblivion of desire and passion she'd never felt before. She held on tighter to him, as if he was rescuing her from the drowning abyss she was in. Yasmine met his fervent kisses with strokes of her tongue intertwined with his in a seductive dance that was in perfect sync.

Cannon pulled away from her lips and trailed kisses down her neck to her collarbone, breaking such an intense sigh from her that she didn't recognize her own voice.

His mouth possessed hers once more, except this time his kisses were a sweet caress across her lips.

"Cannon … " she whispered.

"I love to hear you say my name. I don't think anyone has ever said it quite the way you do."

She giggled, and he placed a tender kiss to her forehead before pulling away from her. She looked around the parking lot and realized two of the cars that had been there when they arrived had left.

"Maybe we should go inside," she said, grabbing her purse.

"Good idea. I think we just gave some of your neighbors a show."

CHAPTER FOUR

In silence, they walked hand in hand to her door. Yasmine was on cloud nine as she used her other hand to rumble around in her purse for her keys. However, she stopped in her tracks as they walked up the sidewalk to her apartment.

"Wait." She put her hand in front of him but kept her eyes on the door of her apartment.

"Yasmine, I promise I'm not going to try anything. I respect you too much."

She shook her head. "No. I always leave on the lamp in the living room if I know I'm returning home after dark."

"Maybe you forgot."

"No, I never forget." She took a step backwards and looked around the apartment complex. "It was on when we left." Her hand flew to her mouth. "Oh my goodness! My door is slightly ajar." She felt faint and leaned on Cannon.

He directed her toward his car in a fast walk as he took out his keys and popped the trunk and then unlocked the car. "Get in, lock the door, and call the police." He spoke calmly as he opened the passenger door, handed her his cell phone, and then shut the door. A few seconds later, he slammed the trunk and rushed up the sidewalk with a crow bar as she nervously dialed the police.

Her heart raced as she waited for Cannon to come out of her apartment. Ten minutes later, she saw the light flick on in her living room and Cannon in the doorway, crow bar still in his hand, with a grip on the shoulder of a struggling teenaged-aged boy.

Yasmine stepped out of the car as Cannon walked down the sidewalk with an intense expression of anger pasted on his face.

"Let me go, you son of a bitch," the teenager yelled at Cannon.

"I'll let you go soon as the police get here."

Yasmine looked closer at the teenager and realized she knew him. He lived in the next building over. A police car with sirens blaring pulled into the parking lot and two police officers stepped out and walked briskly toward them. Some of her neighbors began to assemble outside of their apartments as well.

"Ricky, why did you break into my apartment?" Yasmine's heart was saddened to know he'd tried to steal from her. She was always so nice to him and his baby sister.

"I didn't," he snapped in anger.

Cannon tightened his grip on the boy's shoulder as the boy tried to yank away when the police arrived.

"You didn't? Well explain to me why you were rummaging through Ms. Dubose's jewelry box, and I found this watch in your pocket?" Cannon held up a men's watch that belong to her father.

"I ain't got to tell you nothing." He jerked away, and Cannon let him go. The boy tried to run, but one of the officers grabbed him while the other placed the handcuffs on him.

"No, but you do have to tell us," the police officer said as he locked the cuffs on Ricky's wrists.

"And me," a woman yelled as she walked between Cannon and Yasmine and stood in front of Ricky.

"Mom!"

"How dare you break into Ms. Dubose's home," she snapped as he hung his head in shame. "Is this the first time or are you a part of the group of robbers everyone has been complaining about for the past few months, and you finally got caught?" She jerked his head up. "Look at me when I'm talking to you. Why, Ricky? Why?" She placed her hands on either side of her son's face with tears rolling down hers.

Yasmine's heart broke for her. True, Yasmine was upset that her apartment was broken into, but she knew how hard Ricky's mom worked to provide for him and his sister.

"Do you want to go back to juvy, because that's where they're taking you?" She looked at the police officer that was holding him. "Get him out of my sight." She turned away with a look of disgust.

"Let's go, kid," the officer said, taking Ricky toward the squad car. His mother apologized to Yasmine before walking toward her apartment with a group of women trying to comfort her.

The other officer questioned them about what had happened, as well as a few neighbors who thought there might be some other boys involved. Thirty minutes later, she sat in Cannon's lap on her couch. His warm embrace made her feel more protected and secure than the new locks that the on-call maintenance guy had just changed. She rested her head on Cannon's chest as he rubbed her back.

"Thank you for being here with me," she whispered, resting her head on his shoulder.

"Shhh ... just relax. It's over now."

She sat up to look at him. "You took a risk coming in here to look for the burglar. What if he'd had a gun?"

"I wasn't thinking about that. I just wanted to beat the crap out of whoever had the audacity to break into my girl's place."

My girl? She smiled at his words. She'd wanted to be *his girl* since her freshman year of high school. They'd only been on one date and experienced a surreal kiss, so she was sure he didn't mean it like that, but at least he wanted to protect her.

"Now you see why I'm ready to move?" She slid off of his lap onto the couch.

"When is your lease up?"

"Next summer."

"A frat brother of mine is an attorney. I'll call him in the morning and see what he can do. I'll need to send him a copy of your lease. You shouldn't have to stay in an unsafe environment. You've got noisy college students and now a group of teenagers who think it's okay to break into people's home in the same area where they live."

"But I still need to find another apartment to live in if I'm even able to get out of my lease without having to pay the fee."

"You know what? Doug is moving to New York soon and wants to rent out his townhome instead of selling it. It's really nice. Three story, two car garage, three bedrooms, and two and a half baths. Close to downtown and not far from where you work. I can see what he's renting it for if you're interested. Maybe we can swing by there tomorrow."

"Cannon, that's very sweet of you, but so much has happened tonight. I can't think right now." She closed her eyes and rested her head on the back of the couch.

"I understand. I'll handle it. In the meantime, you can't stay here. Pack a bag. You're coming home with me tonight."

Her eyes shot open and settled on his serious face. "Cannon, I can't do that."

"Yes, you can … and you will. I'd be worried sick knowing you're here alone."

"But he was arrested."

"I know, but he lives in this complex, and he isn't the only one. He's just the only one that got caught."

"Cannon ... I just want to get some rest."

"And you will. Raven is at her boyfriend's place this weekend, so you'll have some peace and quiet. She took her yappy Pomeranian with her, and you can sleep in my room. I'll sleep on the couch."

"Cannon ... " her voice trailed off. She knew he wasn't budging on his decision.

"Grab your things and pack enough for the next few days. I'm not leaving you here. You can follow me in your car."

Realizing he was serious, she leaned over and kissed him on his cheek. "Thank you."

An hour later, he was showing her his bedroom in the ranch-styled home. She had to chuckle inside at the thought she was sleeping in Cannon's bed on the first date. Of course, he would be on the couch, but she'd broken another dating rule: Never go home with the guy on the first date.

After she took a shower in the adjoining bathroom, she put on the blue pajama shirt Cannon had laid on the bed. In her haste to pack, she'd forgotten to throw a nightgown into her suitcase. Wearing his shirt made her feel secure and protected, even if it was three sizes too big for her. She climbed into bed and sipped on the tea Cannon had kindly left on the nightstand. She let its warmth soothe her, even though a glass of wine would've been even better.

A light knock sounded on the door.

"Come in."

When Cannon entered, he was wearing the pajama bottoms that matched the shirt she was wearing along with a white Meharry t-shirt.

"Do you need anything?" he asked, standing in the doorway.

"No, I'm fine. You've been the perfect host."

"Thank you. I'm going to let you get some rest." He turned to go.

"Cannon?"

"Yes."

"I'm still pretty shaken up. Is it possible you can sleep in here instead of on the couch? It's a king-sized bed, so there's plenty of room."

He hesitated for a moment, as if he was going to say no, and she regretted asking him.

"Of course. I'm going to make sure the house is secure and turn off my laptop. I'll be right back."

Yasmine drank the rest of her tea and then slid underneath the fluffy covers. The last thing she remembered before drifting off into a deep slumber, was a tender kiss to her forehead and Cannon whispering, "Good night, Angel face." Then he gathered her in his warm embrace.

During the next three weeks, Cannon's attorney friend was able to get Yasmine out of her apartment lease without having to pay the cancellation fee. She was also able to move into Doug's townhouse, for not much more than what she was paying for her apartment. Yasmine was excited about her new home because she was doing a lease with the possible intention to buy after a year. She was even more excited about spending time with Cannon. After work, she would rush home and cook dinner in her new gourmet kitchen. Then she would wait for Cannon, who would come over after his last class.

Today, she'd stopped by a furniture store with Sherika to browse for bedroom sets. Yasmine was going to move hers into the guestroom and purchase a new one for the master bedroom. Cannon was supposed to meet her for dinner at their favorite spot followed by a movie at six. She was quite surprised at all of the time he was spending with her when she thought he should be studying with his classmates and not at her kitchen table. She couldn't think of the last time he'd mentioned having a study group unless it was during the day.

"This is a nice bed," Yasmine said as they stopped in front of a walnut, four-poster, queen-sized bed.

"Yep. Big enough for you and Cannon when he spends the night," Sherika said, running her hand along a post.

"He doesn't really spend the night. Well ... he does sort of, but he doesn't sleep. I think he's a night owl or has insomnia. When I go to bed, he stays up and studies in the kitchen. When I wake up in the morning, he's gone—at least on the weeknights. On the weekends, he'll crawl into the bed around one, and in the morning, he makes me breakfast or we make it together."

"Awww ... how sweet. But you still haven't—"

"No. That topic hasn't come up. We kiss all the time, we cuddle. He's so affectionate and thoughtful, but he hasn't tried to have sex with me. However, I know he wants to because sometimes when he's hugging me from behind, I can feel a slight erection. And girl, don't get me started on the spot on the back of my neck I never knew existed."

"Oh really?"

"Girl, I don't know what he does with his tongue and lips back there, but I have a mini orgasm from whatever he's doing. It's so freaking erotic."

"Well, since you're buying a new bed, you should test it out," Sherika teased, sitting on the edge of the bed and pouncing up and down on it. "The mattress is quite comfy and has just enough spring action."

The ladies laughed.

"Girl, you're a mess. I do like this one, but it's out of my price range. I'm going to get the sleigh bed with the matching dresser and end table."

"Good decision." Sherika hopped off the bed. "Let's go find that cute salesman that spoke to us when we walked in."

"You just want his phone number."

"If I'm lucky." Sherika winked.

Cannon sat across from Yasmine at her kitchen table while she graded papers. They'd been dating for over a month now, and he'd never felt so relaxed with a woman in such a short time frame. She'd made him take breaks and just have fun. He'd lived in Nashville for almost two years and had never ventured out much as far as site seeing because he was there for medical school. Thanks to her spontaneous nature, they'd been to the Cheekwood Botanical Gardens, the Nashville Zoo, and the Opryland Museum. She'd suggested a country music concert just for the fun of it, but instead they went to a traveling carnival where he felt like a kid again eating corn dogs and funnel cakes as well as riding roller coasters and Ferris wheels.

He was supposed to be studying for an upcoming test on Monday about anatomy, but he was more concerned about her anatomy. His eyes kept straying to her face, and inhaling her perfume that smelled like a mixture of apples and pears. When she'd returned downstairs from her shower earlier, he'd been mesmerized by her mint-green nightgown, which was why he could no longer concentrate. It wasn't sexy lingerie, but it was hot on her with spaghetti straps that kept falling off of her soft shoulders and little pink ribbons around the hem that stopped mid thigh. Before she sat back down, she'd dropped her red pen and bent over to pick it up, exposing pink boy shorts that fit her cute butt like a glove and toned thighs he needed to get in between.

"Shouldn't you be studying?" Yasmine asked with her reading glasses pulled down on her nose.

"I am. I could study you all day and all night and never get tired."

"I can believe that since you never sleep." She closed her folder of graded papers and took off her glasses.

"I know. I guess when I start my residency in a few years, I'll be able to stay up all night. Maybe even pull a double."

She smiled and said softly, "I'm glad you're here." She rose from the table. "I'm still trying to get used to this townhouse. Do you want some more coffee?"

He wanted something all right, and it damn sure wasn't coffee. He wanted her on the kitchen table, on the island, against the wall, on the chair. Wherever she would let him have her so he could hear her soft moans when he was slow and gentle and her passionate screams when he was fast and rough.

No, I can't. Not yet. Too soon. Right? Everything with her felt right and grounded, but he didn't want to rush things.

Before he could consult his conscience any further, she placed her gaze on him and gave him a smile so amazing that any other questions he may have had for himself were thrown out the window. He needed her with a hunger so fierce it shook him.

Driven on a steadfast urge, he went to her and crushed her to him so fast, she let out a startled moan that he quickly muffled with his lips.

He kissed her hard, taunting her lips with his; her mouth succulent and soft. He was in control of their kiss, overpowering her warm, willing mouth as she sighed against his lips and reached for his head to pull him further into her. The moment their lips touched, all the reasons why he shouldn't proceed escaped him. Instead, all of the explanations why he should make love to her overtook him and blazed within him so deep, it created a surge that rippled through his being and into her.

She responded to his kiss as if she'd been waiting for this moment to happen as well. He loved how perfect she felt in his embrace, her soft hands caressing his face and neck. He deepened the kiss even more, and she shuddered, letting out a muffled moan while her mouth vibrated against his. Heat flared in his gut, and he let out a profound groan while an intense flood of aching desire completely consumed him. He was finding it impossible to stop.

Cannon had never known a woman like this. He'd never been so infatuated with a woman's scent, her lips, her warmth, or the way she moaned his name while he feasted on her. He hadn't meant to kiss her so wild, but she was consuming his mind and heart with a need and passion so strong he had to show her what she was doing to him. Her sensual moans escalated his arousal, which was pressed against her stomach, desperate to get inside of her.

"I want you, Yasmine," he whispered in between roaming his tongue around hers.

"Perfect, because I want you, too."

CHAPTER FIVE

Yasmine was lost, falling into an unconsciousness of emotions and passion that charged through her body so hard she could barely stand as he held her against the door of her bedroom. She'd wanted him, too; longer than he'd realized. She had so much pent up desire for him, she didn't know how she would control herself. He wasn't her first, but this was the first time she'd ever felt this needed by a man, and she was going to show him just how much he was needed as well.

His tongue continued a wicked performance with hers, urging her lips further apart while he caressed his hands along her body. Cannon knew exactly what he was doing, as if he owned her body, taking her higher with raw pleasure. She wished he could kiss her forever, but she wanted more than just mind blowing kisses.

"You taste so sweet," he whispered into her mouth. He bent and kissed the top of her shoulder as he eased the strap of her nightgown off, followed by the other strap. The flimsy material fell to the floor, followed by her panties.

"Not fair. You still have on clothes."

"Well then," he began, as he moved her hand down to the top of his jeans and locked his eyes on hers, "take them off."

She obliged, unfastening the button and then unzipping the jeans over a very hard erection. He pulled his t-shirt over his head to expose his smooth, rippled chest and abs. She ran a hand along his chest as he stepped out of his jeans, followed by his boxer shorts. And then that's when she saw what had been rubbing against her through his jeans. She knew it would be big, but damn, she wasn't prepared for all of that. She gulped. His first name was definitely appropriate.

"Better?" he asked.

"Mmmm … much."

"And you'll be fine," he said with a cocky grin as he glanced down at his erection and then back to her face.

In one swoop, he picked her up and carried her to the bed while he continued to lavish kisses on her. His mouth devoured hers, which sent shivers of anticipation through her for what was to come next. Lying beside her, he trailed his tongue along her neck while his hand wandered down her body and stopped at her waiting center. His gaze fell on her face when he entered her with one finger, causing her to whimper an unfamiliar sound and suck in her breath. He kissed her lightly on the lips as he stroked in and out of her slowly.

His eyes darkened as he continued pleasuring her with his fingers, while his other hand gripped her hip. He didn't say anything or move, just stared at her with an expression so intense she was almost scared. She placed a hand on the chiseled perfection of his handsome face, and he bent down to kiss her as she felt her first orgasm burn through her body. An inferno was blazing on her skin, and he caused it.

"Please, Cannon. I'm so ready for you."

"I know you are, Angel face."

She smiled when he called her by her nickname and reached up to kiss him, pulling him fully on top of her.

"Wait, Yasmine," he said, lifting off of her. She watched as he retreated to the drawer of her dresser that he used when he spent the night. Cannon lit the two candles sitting on her dresser, pulled out a small box, and brought it back to the bed. He set it on the nightstand and turned off the lamp, letting the candles set a romantic mood.

He began trailing kisses from her neck down to her breasts. He sucked one taut nipple between his lips, swirling his tongue around it before taking it deep into his mouth once more. Yasmine held onto his head as pleasure-filled moans escaped her while he assaulted her breasts back and forth. His hand roamed down her body, and she parted her thighs as his hand palmed her center that was growing impatient with having to wait for the real thing. The passion building inside of her was ready to explode all over him, and she jerked his hand down to her slick opening as he entered a finger into her. His lips left her breasts and continued a trail down to her belly button and then to the soft nestle of curls. His tongue replaced his finger, and she gripped his shoulders hard when he buried his face into her, licking and kissing her other lips senseless. She tried to hold back an orgasm because his tongue felt so damn good, but she couldn't control the sensations racing through her veins, and she shuddered hard as his tongue darted faster in and out of her.

"Cannon, I don't think I have any more left in me."

He rolled off of the bed and opened the box on the nightstand. "Yes, you do. That was only a teaser."

After he placed on a condom, he rejoined her on the bed and pulled her underneath him. His hands tightened on her hips, sinking her into the bed, and raising her legs around him. She gasped as inch by inch of hardened heat entered into her. She met his gaze, dark with desire and tried to move, but he held her still.

Sliding her hands down his chest, and over muscles tight with tension, she finally circled around to his back. He began to move slowly, as he still worked a few more inches inside of her, and she wiggled to adjust to him. His hands tightened on her butt, pulling her closer to him; she moved her body up to his, wanting him deeper and deeper, where she could feel him all the way. She clutched his head, tangling her fingers into his soft curls. Her eyes fluttered shut as more fervent passion swept through her with each deepened thrust. Her words were incoherent as her pleadings escaped her, crying out as her body trembled under his. The pleasure he caused invaded her mind and spirit, and although she tried to fight it, it was no use. So she gave up and let the tidal wave of ecstasy slam through her body and senses.

Cannon held her tightly against him as she had another orgasm. He was trying his best not to do the same, but she was making him dizzy with her moans of pleasure and feminine scent radiating in the air. He wanted to savor his first time with her with what little control he did have left, and it wasn't much. Something had possessed his body, heart and mind, and he found himself sinking further into her soul with an intensity that he couldn't explain.

There was something about her that set him off balance as her femininity enveloped him, her inner muscles tightening with each thrust. Her hands clenched his shoulders and her legs gripped his waist as she let go of another powerful scream. He couldn't take it anymore. He felt himself exploding, his pace faster and uncontrollable, as he unleashed into her, pounding her into the mattress. He let out a roar and a few curse words before he fell exhausted, but satisfied, on top of her.

A while after Yasmine had fallen asleep, he lay there holding her to his chest with their legs intertwined. They'd made love two more times, each time more intense than the one before. Poor thing, she nearly crawled to the bathroom, laughing the entire way, after the second time. After the third, she barely kissed him before crashing onto his chest where she was now resting peacefully. And for the first time in a long while, he was resting peacefully as well.

His mother had always called him a busy bee. He was one to never be idle for long, always finding something to get into; whether it was school work, community service projects, or helping out a friend in need. Sure, he was focused and goal-oriented. An intellect, according to his family and friends, even though he never saw it that way. He just liked to learn about new things and tended to express himself differently from others. Activities outside of academics never caused a problem with his study habits. Even though lately, he found himself not wanting to study. Instead, he found himself wanting to be with the woman who had made him realize it was okay to appreciate life. He'd had girlfriends, and friends-with-benefits, in high school and in his undergrad years at Morehouse, but nothing serious because his focus was getting into medical school. But with Yasmine, he knew this time it was different.

She stirred and lifted her head.

"Are you going to blow out the candles?" she asked sleepily.

He kissed the top of her forehead. "In a minute. I just want to stare at you. I told you I could look at you all day and night."

She giggled and kissed his chest. "I know, but it's three in the morning. I prefer you get some rest."

"I am. Just holding you is relaxing. Thank you, Yasmine."

"For what?"

"For making me realize I need to slow down."

"Well ... I wish my father had. I think that's why I'm so adamant about you taking some time for yourself. I'm not saying cut something out of your schedule or your life, but its okay to stop and smell the roses every once in awhile."

He sniffed her neck and exhaled. "I smell one right now." Laughing, he patted her butt.

Yasmine rubbed the scar on the left side of his chest, circling it with her fingernail.

"How did you get this scar?"

"I had stitches there years ago."

"What happened?"

"I was about twelve, riding my bike and trying to race Raven down the street. I lost my balance, fell over and crashed hard into the sidewalk and falling on the handle bar. Raven rushed home to get my father. Luckily, he's a doctor so he knew what to do. My mom's a doctor, too, but she was too busy crying. Dad said if the gash had been a few inches deeper, it would've pierced my heart, and I could've bled to death."

Yasmine sat up and looked at him with wistful eyes. She kissed his forehead, his nose, his lips, and then the scar.

"I'm glad you didn't. That would've been the most horrible thing in the world not to have known you."

"You're too sweet. What would I do without you?"

"Well, for one thing, you wouldn't be resting and relaxing right now. You'd probably be wide awake trying to figure out how to save the world."

He chuckled. "Oh, speaking of which—"

"—what brainstorm is going on up there now?" she asked, tapping his head with her finger.

"I spoke to the officer that arrested Ricky, and he referred me to his social worker. When Ricky gets out of juvenile detention in a few weeks, I want to start mentoring him as a part of my fraternity's big brother program. I spoke to his mother a few days ago about it."

She smiled and kissed him on his scar. "You are the epitome of a good man."

"Thank you." He pulled her on top of him. "Are you ready for round four?"

"All right, boys and girls, you did an excellent job in dress rehearsal today, so I know you'll be awesome tonight." Yasmine stood with her students in the hallway, giving them a last minute pep talk before they were to go inside of the cafeteria for the Holiday Extravaganza. Her students, who were dressed as reindeers and snowflakes, were lined up and anxious to perform. Yasmine kept looking around. Cannon had promised to come, but he was running late. She wasn't surprised at his lateness, but she was surprised he hadn't called. Lately, he seemed on edge about something, but whenever she asked, he said everything was fine.

Yasmine was definitely seeing some of the same signs her father displayed when he was working overtime and stressed. She'd promised herself she would never date a workaholic; unfortunately, not only was she dating one, Cannon was also a perfectionist. Her cell phone vibrating in her Mrs. Clause apron interrupted her thoughts. It was Cannon.

"Hey, baby," she whispered into the phone. "Where are you?"

"I'm not going to be able to make the play, Angel face."

She sighed, looked to her left, and motioned for Sherika to watch her class. Yasmine walked out of the side door that led to the back parking lot.

"Is something wrong?" she asked.

"No. I just have some things to do."

"Oh something came up all of a sudden? Because you said this morning you were available."

"I just can't come, so drop it," he fussed.

"Excuse me. Who are you snapping at?"

He sighed. "I'm sorry. I just have some things on my mind right now."

"Is there anything I can do?"

"No, beautiful. I'm sorry again for snapping. I just need to take care of something."

"Will I see you later on?"

"Probably not. I gotta go, Yaz."

"Me, too. The kiddies go on stage in a few."

She hung up before he could say anything else. She wasn't sure what could possibly be bothering him. She could tell something was wrong the other day when he came over, barely said a word, and stayed in the kitchen until four in the morning, going over a study guide for an exam. And when she'd asked what he got on his midterm paper, he'd grunted and said everything was fine. Yasmine wasn't up to dealing with his sudden mood swings. However, she decided she would give him some space, and if he wanted to talk about whatever the heck was bothering him, she'd listen.

CHAPTER SIX

Yasmine looked at the clock. Cannon had promised to be at her home at five so they could go bowling. It was now six, and he hadn't called to say he was running late. For the past several days, since the Holiday Extravaganza, he'd seemed distant and preoccupied. But whenever she asked, he said he was fine. He'd even broken two dates, which she didn't mind because she knew finals were coming up for him, but he broke them hours past the designated time as she sat waiting. She had a feeling tonight would be the same since he was an hour late.

At eight, she put on her pajamas, climbed into bed, and tried to watch an Elizabeth Taylor movie she'd seen a dozen times. When the phone rang, she thought surely it was Cannon, but it was a teacher on her grade level calling for some advice on a student.

Fed up, she dialed Cannon's cell number once she hung up with her colleague. He picked up on the sixth ring.

"Hello?" he said in a rushed, whispered tone.

"Hey."

"Um ... hey Yasmine."

"Busy?" She tried to take the attitude out of her tone.

"I'm in a seminar on campus. I just stepped out to take your call."

"I see. Did you forget we had plans tonight?"

"Oh. I completely forgot. Sorry, baby. It's been a long day, and then I found out one of the doctors over the pediatric residents at John Hopkins would be here doing a seminar, and I just had to meet him. John Hopkins is my first choice to do my residency, but I promise to come see you tonight. I have to stop by the food bank on my way to help pack boxes of food for Christmas. What's it been, two days since I've seen my Angel face?"

"Five days. I feel like you're avoiding me, Cannon."

"I'm not avoiding you, but I do have to go. I'll call you before I come. Promise."

Cannon walked into his home after midnight, slammed the door, and threw his book bag down. Then he screamed, "Move," at Raven's dog, Smokey, who barked at Cannon's mean tone.

"Shut the hell up!" Cannon snapped as the dog continued to follow him through the foyer and into the family room, where Raven sat studying and sipping something warm out of her big mug.

"I know you didn't just tell my dog to shut the hell up." She closed her book and looked at Cannon as he crashed next to her on the couch. "What's eating you?"

"Nothing," he said through clenched teeth as Smokey jumped up and sat on his lap. "Sorry, boy." He rubbed the dog's back before he jumped down and ran.

"Oh it's something for you to come home, slam the door, and then curse at my dog."

He shrugged. "I always curse at your dog, you're just usually not home." He laughed as Raven playfully punched him on the shoulder.

"Seriously, Cannon. What's the problem? You've been moody lately, and I'm surprised you're not over at Yasmine's."

"I was supposed to go over there, but when I called, she didn't answer the phone. I believe she's mad at me because I broke our date tonight. I forgot. I've been busy, and she has to understand that."

"And what else? You being busy hasn't been a problem before."

Cannon hesitated. "My grades have fallen since I've been dating Yasmine."

"How bad?"

"I got my first C a few weeks ago on the midterm paper that I rushed through for Dr. Clayton's class. He took off for grammar and errors. My content was fine."

"Not good, Cannon. Not good at all. That paper counted as thirty percent of our grade."

"I know. I have to make an A on the final paper in order to get a B in the class."

"You need to get your priorities straight. Something has to go. Medical school should be your only focus."

"I don't want to break up with Yasmine. She's very special to me."

"I wasn't saying break up with her, silly. Tone down on some of your extracurricular activities, but also explain to her you're in med school. Where did you go after the seminar? I was looking for you to see if you wanted to go to the library to study. Finals are next week."

"I went to the food bank to help make the Christmas boxes."

"Exactly. When you should've been doing research for your last paper or studying for finals."

"I like to help people when I can, Raven. Don't you remember when we were growing up? Mom and Dad always told us to give back. Dad is always doing something for the community, such as his scholarship programs or mentoring to boys without fathers."

"Cannon, you remind me so much of Dad, it's scary. However, he's finished med school and is a heart surgeon … you aren't. You think he'd be happy to know about your C?"

"I hear you, baby sis by five minutes." He added in the five minute part because she hated being called baby sis. She felt as if she was the oldest sibling as well since they were twins.

He knew Raven was right. He kissed his sister on the cheek and took out his cell phone to call Yasmine, hoping she would pick up this time. He retreated to his room as he listened to the rings.

"Hello?" she answered, her voice barely above a whisper. He could tell she'd been crying, and he hated that.

"We need to talk."

"I'm listening."

"In person. Can I come over?"

Yasmine sat on her couch as she waited for Cannon to speak. She was so mad she didn't want to say the wrong thing. Instead, she decided to wait to see what he was going to say first. However, he just sat there staring at her, and it was driving her mad. One, she was mad he'd broken their past few dates and was snappy and moody. But two, it had been a week since they'd made love, and she was turned on by his presence.

"Yasmine, first of all I need to apologize to you for my behavior lately. It doesn't have anything to do with you."

"Okay, what's wrong?" She was terrified to ask a man a question like that after he'd just told her it doesn't have anything to do with you. The last man who said that statement was breaking up with her and dating someone else. She sighed and braced herself for his answer.

"I've been in a foul mood lately because I got a C on my midterm paper; I didn't take my time with it. I rushed through it because I was trying to stop and smell the roses. A few of my other grades have slipped a tad, but I still have A's in those classes. I'm just worried about the final in the class that I made the C."

She stood and placed her hands on her hips. "I know you aren't blaming me for your grades slipping. Maybe you should get your priorities straight and stop taking on extra projects."

He spoke calmly. "Baby, I'm not blaming you for anything. When you asked me what my grade was a few weeks ago, I didn't want to talk about it because I knew in my head I needed to get my act together. You and my sister are right. I've taken on way too many responsibilities, and in the process, I met you and it was like a breath of fresh air. You've taught me how to settle down and relax, and I did just that. Now, I need to focus on medical school."

"Why didn't you just tell me? You've been avoiding me, and when you did talk to me, you were moody and snappy. I don't appreciate you treating me like that."

"Yasmine, I sincerely apologize. I'm used to keeping things to myself, especially negative things. I'm a—"

"—perfectionist," she finished for him.

"Something like that." He grinned. "But, you can't get upset, be mad at me, or think I'm avoiding you. There are times when I'll be busy with studying, assignments, and labs. Next year, I'll be a third-year medical student which means no more classes. I start my rotations at the hospital, which entails long hours. I may not see you every day, but none of that will change the fact that I love you and want to be with you. It just means it's a part of the journey I have to take to be a doctor."

"Cannon, while I understand, it still doesn't give you any excuse to snap at me, ignore me or forget we had plans. Trust me. There are plenty of men wanting to take your place and get at all of this." She motioned her hand in the air from her head to her feet and back up. She stopped as she replayed what he said in her head. "Wait. Did you say you love me?"

He pulled her back down to the couch and onto his lap. "Yes, Yasmine. Very, very much."

Tears welled in her eyes and began to roll down her cheeks. He wiped them away, but a few more came. "I love you, too. Cannon, I promise I always will."

"I would love to show you right now just how much."

Afterwards, they lay intertwined together as the candle light illuminated her bedroom. She drew circles around his scar. She'd become increasingly obsessed with it every time she saw it.

"Why did you make a C on your paper?"

He sighed. "Errors like typos and grammar, things that I do know. I just rushed through and didn't take my time to thoroughly proofread it In fact, I'm working on a final paper now, which is why I haven't been around much lately. It's pretty much done. Just need to read through it line by line."

"Well, I don't know much about medical content, but I used to work in the Language Arts tutorial lab in college. I can read over your papers for you if you would like."

"I really appreciate that. Thank you." He kissed the top of her forehead.

"That's what girlfriends are for."

"I've missed you, Angel face. I'm sorry for not communicating with you. I know me being a workaholic is upsetting to you, because of your father, and I promise to not take on so many extra things. My main focus is medical school, you, and hopefully getting accepted to John Hopkins for my residency. I'm not saying I'm getting rid of my community service projects, but I just won't sign up for so many around crunch time. Plus, once I start my rotations, I won't have time.

"Are you busy now?"

"Nope. What did you have in mind?" He kissed her softly on the lips.

"I was going to read your paper for you."

"Too bad. I was going to make love to you, again."

"Or we could do that."

EPILOGUE

Two years later.

"Yasmine?" Cannon called out at the bottom of her staircase. He'd just left the hospital and stopped by his house to pick up some clothes and a few things. He was off for the next two days and had promised to spend them with Yasmine. It was Christmas Eve, and though she still didn't celebrate Christmas anymore, she had allowed him to put up a few decorations including two stockings over the fireplace. He placed a small box into her stocking.

"Coming, Cannon," she called out, as she descended the staircase in a red sweater and jeans with snowflake socks on her feet. She'd let her hair grow longer, and it bounced around her shoulders. She ran to him and jumped up into his arms, placing kisses all over his face.

"You missed me, baby?" He carried her over to the fireplace where she'd set out a blanket with their dinner and wine. He loved their indoor picnics during the winter and had asked her earlier to set one up for them.

"Of course."

"I have some very important news to share with you, Yaz."

Her eyes lit up at his words, and he could tell she was anxious to know. He pulled out an envelope from his back pocket and handed it to her, as her eyes perused the address.

"John Hopkins?" She looked at him, and back at the envelope, as she took out the letter he'd already read a dozen times. She read it silently in her head, but her face didn't light up as he expected. When she did look up, he saw her eyes welled with tears. "You got accepted to John … Hopkins for your residency program way in Baltimore. Congrats, babe."

She smiled, but it wasn't the beautiful smile he was used to, and he knew why.

"Thank you. I couldn't believe it when I saw the letter in the mailbox yesterday. I was in shock for the longest and then on complete cloud nine today at the hospital, but you're the first person I've told."

"Really? What about your Dad? I know he would definitely want to know."

"I'll tell the family when we go to Memphis for New Year's."

"So you're definitely going to John Hopkins."

"Of course. Why wouldn't I?"

"I just thought you were considering Meharry Hospital."

"I've considered a lot of things in the past few days, but no matter where I decide to do my residency—whether it's here, Hopkins, or Purdue, you'll be with me. That is, if you want to go."

"Wait. What?"

He stood, took the box out her stocking, and knelt in front of her.

"Oh my goodness." Tears ran down her cheeks as he opened the small black velvet box.

"Yasmine Dubose, I love you. I want to spend my life with you, waking up every morning to your angelic face and beautiful smile. Please say you'll give me the honor of being my wife, Angel face." He slipped the one carat, princess-cut diamond on her left ring finger and then wiped away her tears.

"Yes, Cannon. I would love to be your wife, and I'll go anywhere you want me to just as long as we're together."

What was supposed to be a kiss turned into more as they made love in front of the fireplace. Afterwards, she laid on top him, twirling her finger around his scar as always.

"When do you want to get married?" he asked.

"How about this summer before we move to Baltimore? We can get married in Memphis since that's where most of our family is located."

"This summer it is. Whatever you want, Yasmine. I won't be able to help much with the planning."

"No problem. You just leave everything to me. I'm sure my mom and Sherika will be happy to help me. All I need you to do is show up."

"There's no place I'd rather be than with you." He kissed her lightly and turned her over on her back as she giggled and gave him her simply amazing smile.

PART TWO

PROLOGUE

2 months later...

Cannon pulled his Mustang into the driveway of his fiancée's townhome and slammed on the brakes to avoid hitting the garage door. He'd sped the majority of the way because he couldn't wait to share his exciting news with her. Grabbing his overnight bag and the envelope sitting on top of it from the passenger seat, he rushed to the front door, fumbling with the keys before he finally managed to get in.

"Yasmine!" he called out as he barely stepped foot into the foyer, tossing the bag on the hardwood floor but held onto the envelope that burned in his hand. He was so elated, he couldn't contain it. She had always been supportive in whatever he decided to do, so he knew she had to be the first person he shared his life-changing news with.

His eyes perused the living area. Bridal magazines were spread out in front of the lit fireplace along with pictures of cakes, wedding dresses, and samples of invitations. She had decided that would be the perfect place to sit and plan their wedding since that's where he'd proposed two months ago on Christmas Eve. He smiled as he remembered the loving expression on her face with tears streaming down her cheeks as she said yes.

He rushed up the stairs—his long legs skipping every other step—to her bedroom, laughing when he heard the shower running and her screaming in a falsetto at the top of her lungs along with Prince's "Kiss" on the radio. Yasmine couldn't sing a note, but her bubbly and carefree personality always warmed his heart. Little things like singing off-key in the shower made him remember why he was in love with her. He dropped the envelope on the vanity and pulled the shower curtain back. She stopped singing "I wanna be your fantasy" in mid-sentence and gasped as her brown, doe-like eyes rested on him.

"You scared me, Cannon!" She flicked water on him playfully and yanked the shower curtain shut.

"Sorry, Angel face." He reopened it to admire her naked body as she stood under the shower stream to rinse off her melon scented soap. His manhood stirred as the water glistened on her caramel-coated skin and ran over places he wanted to kiss and touch. "You need some help?" His voice laced with seduction.

"No, baby. I'm done." She shut off the water, and he lifted her out of the tub. He began to dry her off with a towel as she continued to talk a mile a minute. "Besides, we have to be out of here in thirty minutes. We have dinner reservations, so hurry up and get out of those scrubs. Oh, and happy Valentine's Day." She kissed him on his cheek before walking toward the closet.

Cannon was in his last semester of Meharry Medical School and had just gotten off from doing a double shift at the hospital. He didn't have time to change at home, especially when the envelope arrived. He'd read the letter almost five times before it hit him that what he had worked so hard for during the past two years was actually going to happen.

"Cannon, we really need to finish discussing the wedding plans," she called out from the closet. "It's February, and we only have five more months. I'll bring the wedding notes with us." They'd decided to get married a month after he graduated from medical school and then move to Baltimore, Maryland, where Cannon was to begin his pediatric residency at John Hopkins Hospital.

"Oh and guess what?" she paused, peeking her head out of the closet before going back in. "The music teacher at my school is available to play during the wedding. His piano rendition of "Ribbon in the Sky" is so overwhelming. He played and sung it today after work for me, and I teared up, which means I'll be bawling at the wedding."

"Um ... that's great, Yaz."

She stepped back out in a short, fitted hot pink dress and looked taken aback to see he still stood there in his scrubs.

With her hands on her hips and a little pout she said, "Babe, hurry up."

"It doesn't take me long to shower and get dressed. But first, read this." He handed her the envelope from the counter and walked around to zip up her dress. She opened the envelope as his hands encircled her waist, and he rested his chin on her shoulder to look over it as he re-read the letter.

"Oh my goodness!" she squealed. "The grant for the Brazil project was approved." She turned around and jumped up and down in his arms, planting kisses all over his face.

"This is wonderful. You worked so hard along with your team to make this happen. No one deserves this more than you, Cannon. Now we have so much to celebrate. Your graduation, the grant proposal, and most importantly our wedding this July." She hugged him again, and he kissed her forehead before letting her go. She turned to the mirror, took off the shower cap, and ran her hands through her straight, shoulder length hair. She had natural curls, but sometimes had them blown out.

"Well … actually, Yasmine, there may be a slight change of plans," he said uneasily, looking at her through the mirror. Her smile faded.

"What type of change?" Her voice went up an octave, and he caught the familiar tremble in her tone whenever he was about to relay some bad news.

"Um … well, I have to leave for Brazil the week after graduation, and I'll be there until possibly next summer to assist Dr. Johnson and the rest of the team in setting everything up."

"No the hell you won't." She turned around to face him. "What are you talking about? You can't be there for a year. You're starting your residency, and we're getting married in July. We've already reserved the church and the reception hall."

"Baby, I know, but I can postpone my residency until next fall, and we can always get married when I get back. You act as if this wasn't a possibility."

"But we've been making plans to get married and go to Baltimore. When do you suggest we get married now?"

"I'm thinking maybe next Christmas Eve, since that's when I proposed. You'll have more time to plan." He stepped toward her, but she moved away, leaning on the counter for support as if she'd just had the wind knocked out of her.

"Cannon, that's almost two years from now."

"Yaz, it really isn't that big of a deal. We can get married anytime, but I can't just go to Brazil anytime. The project starts this summer."

"Excuse me?"

"Yasmine, you know my team and I have been working on this grant for a while. That small village in

Brazil has no real medical services, and by setting up the clinic, we'll be able to provide them with such. You know it's been my goal to help people in need."

"You don't think I know that? I've been supportive of everything you do, but what about us? Our plans? I just voided my contract for the next school year for Nashville City Schools, so I don't have a job in the fall right now and my townhome is on the market."

"I'm sure you could find a job teaching and just take your home off the market."

"I do not believe this." She walked out of the bathroom and into the bedroom with him following her. He reached out to grab her elbow, but she snatched it away. "Don't touch me right now."

He'd never seen so much anger on her angelic face before and it scared him. He'd promised to never make her simply amazing smile go away, but he had, and it wasn't the first time.

"I thought you'd be happy for me," he said quietly. "We can get married any time. This is a once in a lifetime opportunity for me."

"No, marrying *me* is the once in a lifetime opportunity."

"And we will, just not as originally planned." He hesitated, knowing his next words would sting. "It's just a lot going on right now, and I think we should wait on getting married ..." He trailed off as the hurt on her face emerged even more.

"Cannon, my mother and I have already put deposits down. They're non-refundable."

"I'll receive half of my trust fund from my parents when I graduate. I can pay you back."

"So you just don't want to marry me anymore." Her voice cracked and tears rolled down her face. He felt like crap.

"I didn't say that."

"You know what? I'm tired of this. Since we've been together, your work has always been more important than this relationship. You've cancelled dates and vacations because you're always off somewhere doing whatever the hell Cannon wants to do. You've never once considered my feelings, even though I've been supportive of you and your endeavors every step of the way, including that damn grant."

"Yasmine, I'm not saying I don't want to marry you, just not now. We can get married anytime after I return."

"I'm so sick of you saying we can get married anytime, as if marrying me is something to scratch off your extremely long to-do list."

"That's not what I meant." Sliding his hands down his face, he said through clenched teeth, "This isn't easy for me ..."

She walked toward him while slipping off her engagement ring. "I'm going to make it real easy." Her voice choked on the words. "You don't have to worry about marrying me, and you can go pursue your *once in a lifetime opportunity*." She slapped the ring in his hand and turned back toward the bathroom, unzipping her dress. "I'm done."

"You're calling off our engagement?" he asked in shock as he walked behind her. He grabbed her to him, searching for some type of familiarity on her face, but all he saw was the pain and frustration that he had caused *again*.

"No," she screamed in a tone he'd never heard before. She pushed his chest, and he let go. "I'm calling off this relationship that you've barely been in."

"That's not true. I love you very much."

"I can't tell." She opened the drawer to the vanity that held the things he used when he spent the night and began tossing them into a bag on the counter. "I suggest you get your things out of the dresser drawer before I burn them Bernadette style from *Waiting to Exhale*." She turned toward the closet.

"Yasmine, don't … don't do this." He felt the emotions in him rise. She came out with his clothes and started throwing them at him. They hit his chest before landing in a puddle at his feet. However, the second batch of clothes confused him. They were sundresses, shorts, and tops. "These aren't mine."

"I know, but you bought them for me to wear on our honeymoon, and I don't want or need them anymore." She threw them with the rest of the clothes on the bathroom floor.

Grabbing her by the wrists, he pulled her hard to him. She tried to squirm away, but he held her firmly to his chest. She huffed and puffed with her eyes fixated on the wall behind him.

"Look at me, woman!" He held both of her wrists in one hand and turned her face up to his with the other. "I love you. Don't do this, Angel face," he pleaded.

"Let me go," she screamed at the top of her lungs with tears rolling down her face. She pushed her body hard against him, and he let go of her wrists. "Please leave."

"You don't mean it."

"Just go save the world, Cannon," she said sarcastically.

Grabbing the bag on the counter, he gathered up his clothes on the floor, leaving hers there. He turned to look at her and the hurt on her face was too much for his heart to bear. Tears stained her cheeks, and she shook uncontrollably. He wanted to reach out and hold her, console her, but the expression on her face screamed stay away from me.

"You'll regret this one day," he said as he walked down the stairs with her following him.

"The only thing I regret is wasting two years with you." Her voice was cold with no emotion. She picked up the vase of red roses from the foyer table that he'd sent that day to her school and threw them just as he closed the front door. He heard it crash on the other side and a loud, sobbing scream from her.

CHAPTER ONE

12 years later ...

Yasmine dropped her briefcase and purse on the couch on the way to the ringing phone in the kitchen. She grabbed it and saw Sherika Williams, her best friend's name on the caller ID.

"Hey, lady!" Walking to the refrigerator, she noticed a note under a magnet from her mother. Yasmine shook her head. Why didn't her mother just text her? They both had iPhones. She pulled out a chicken and vegetable stir-fry she'd made yesterday and raked it into a plate. She hadn't eaten since that morning. It was now late evening, and she was famished.

"Yaz, I had the best Valentine's Day ever yesterday!" Sherika squealed.

"What romantic thing did Doug do now?" She glanced at the note.

Will be home late. Out on a date with you know who.

"He asked me to marry him!" Sherika squeaked, and Yasmine imagined her friend jumping up and down at the same time.

She closed the microwave door and pushed two minutes on the panel. "That's wonderful! I knew it wouldn't be long before he did. You two have been great friends over the years, and have always had a crush on each other. I was glad when you finally reconnected in the same city last year. I knew it would only be a matter of time before he popped the question!"

"Me too! I never wanted to do the long distance thing, but I'm glad we've always remained friends. But when he moved here, it just felt right."

"How did he propose? I want all of the details."

"He surprised me in my classroom at the end of the day and whisked me off to Montreal. He got permission from my principal so I could be off for the rest of the week. We're here now."

"In Canada?"

"Yep. He's here for business, so he's actually in a meeting at the moment. I just couldn't believe it."

"So when's the big day?" Taking off her black suit jacket, Yasmine tossed it on a barstool next to the island.

"Well ... we have to get married really soon, like the first weekend in June. He's accepted a job in Madrid, Spain."

"Congratulations. I'll start looking for plane tickets to New York. Just tell me when."

"Since my family is mostly in Memphis and his is in St. Louis, we're going to get married in Memphis."

"Makes sense." The microwave beeped. Yasmine took out the plate, poured a glass of Merlot, and carried the items to the couch, plopping down on it.

"And you have to be my maid of honor."

"I would be honored."

"Thank you, girl. And I need a big favor. Because I'm in New York, there are some things with the planning process that I can't do, even though I just secured a wedding coordinator in Memphis. I need someone there I know and trust, and I trust you."

"Of course I will. Lucky for you, my consulting contract with the school system doesn't end until the middle of June, so I'll be here. Just email me the information and a laundry list of assignments, and I'll get on it."

Having lived away from her hometown of Memphis since she was eighteen, Yasmine had moved back temporarily six months ago from Atlanta to be with her mother, who was in remission from stage one breast cancer after completing her rounds of chemotherapy.

"Perfect. Doug has asked his best man to help with some things like the tuxedos and what not."

At the mention of the best man, Yasmine's heart dropped and the food on her plate no longer looked appetizing. She took a sip of her wine before asking the dreaded question.

"Who's the best man?"

"Relax, its Doug's big brother. He lives in St. Louis and will go with you to the first meeting with the coordinator this Monday at three o'clock if you can make it."

Yasmine breathed easy again and took a sip of her wine.

"I can make it. I honestly thought you were going to say someone else's name."

"Nope. Doug did ask him, but he's speaking at a medical convention in Vegas that weekend and won't be able to come to the wedding."

"Why am I not surprised that Dr. Cannon Arrington is too busy to attend his best friend's wedding?"

"I can't believe you haven't bumped into him since you've been back in Memphis."

"Fortunately, no. Besides, I've been with mother or doing consulting work for the school system."

"Doug said Cannon has been in Brazil the past few months doing business for Doctors Unlimited. You know he's the CEO of the organization. He's in and out of town, so maybe that's why you haven't run into him."

"Sherika, what is our agreement?"

Her best friend since fifth grade sighed. "That I never mention *him* or what he's doing to you."

"Thank you. Now back to you and the fabulous wedding I'm going to help plan."

The ladies talked for a few more moments about the wedding details until Doug returned from his meeting and Sherika happily got off the phone. Yasmine finished her dinner in relief mode. The last thing she wanted to do was to run into Cannon, much less plan a wedding with him. Even though she was now thirty-six and not the naïve girl she was in her early twenties when she thought she was in love, she still didn't want to see him. It took her years to get over their relationship that she thought was perfect. Eventually she'd dated again, and even had a few marriage proposals, but turned them all down. They had been nice guys, but she'd guarded her heart to the point of never falling in love again, dumping guys left and right when she thought they wanted a permanent relationship.

Yasmine glanced over the notes for the wedding she jotted down and breathed another sigh of relief that Cannon wouldn't be the best man.

"Make sure to give her the medicine twice a day with food." Cannon scribbled out a prescription for strep throat on his pad and handed it to his patient's mother. "She'll need to rest for the rest of the week, so I'm giving you a doctor's note for her school as well." He handed her another piece of paper.

"Thank you so much, Dr. Arrington. I'm glad you were able to squeeze us in today."

"No problem. I've been your children's pediatrician for years. I care about their well-being and your peace of mind." He looked at the little girl who sat on the exam table, leaning her head on her mother's shoulder. "Kailyn, make sure to grab something from the treasure box by the door."

The little girl smiled and slid off of the table. "You're my favorite doctor," she said with a hoarse voice as she sat on the floor rummaging through the box.

After they left, Cannon washed his hands and headed back to his office. He checked his watch. It was almost two o'clock, and he needed to head to the other side of town. He chuckled. He couldn't believe he agreed to be Doug's best man that morning, but since he'd gotten the week of the medical conference mixed up, he was now available. Plus, Doug's brother was a truck driver and would be in and out of town, making it hard for him to run whatever errands the groom needed.

Cannon hung his white coat on the back of the door and retrieved his blue suit jacket from his desk chair and took a deep breath. Today he would have to face Yasmine for the first time in twelve years. His heart stopped for a second. Just the thought of her still shook him. Even though he hadn't seen or spoken to her, she'd still entered his mind from time to time. Her smile, her cute giggle, the sexy way his name rolled off her tongue and how she glided her fingers over his chest, all still occupied his brain. He'd hated the way their relationship ended and had felt guilty about it ever since.

"Getting ready to leave?"

Cannon snapped out of his thoughts and looked up to see his twin sister, Raven, standing in his doorway, staring at him with the same almond-shaped, chocolate eyes he saw every morning in the mirror. Her pink peacoat lay draped over her arm, a huge black leather purse dangled on her wrist, and the gray opera gloves lying in her hand matched the belt on her black sheath dress. Her reddish-brown curls were swept up into a bun on top of her head with a few escaped ringlets around her face. He smiled. His sister was always classy and elegant even when she wasn't trying to be.

"Yep." He grabbed his car keys.

"I'll walk out with you. I'm off to the hospital to deliver your next patient."

Cannon and Raven, at age thirty-eight, were the oldest of five siblings. They ran their family's private medical practice, Arrington Family Specialists, which their parents started when the twins were in undergrad. The middle child, Sean, was a psychiatrist, followed by Bria, an allergist who also specialized in holistic medicine, and the youngest, Shelbi, who had just completed her first year of her residency, would eventually join the practice as an endocrinologist. Their parents had recently semi-retired, working only three days a week, and would fully retire once Shelbi completed her residency.

Once they made it to the parking lot, he could sense the hesitancy in Raven as she stood next to his black 745 BMW twirling her keys.

"Soooooo … are you nervous?"

"A little. I'm taken aback that I had no idea she's been in town for six months or that her mother had cancer, but apparently she asked Sherika and Doug not to tell me." He shrugged.

"It won't be so bad. You're just meeting with the coordinator to set up appointments and what not. Plus, you're only responsible for selecting tuxedos and the groom's cake. You really won't have to see her again until the wedding weekend."

"Don't forget I'm planning the bachelor party." He grinned with a wink.

"You should call Rasheed to help you."

"Already did, but he said since he was married to Bria and had a baby on the way, those days were gone. However, he gave me the information I needed and offered his private jet to fly to Vegas."

"Speaking of babies, I gotta run before this one delivers itself." She walked toward her Mercedes. "I'll call you when I have a chance."

Thirty minutes later, Cannon sat in his car in the parking lot of the wedding planner's office, strumming his fingers on the steering wheel. A few cars were there, all of which had Tennessee tags, except a black two door Lexus with Georgia tags and a sorority plate which was the same sorority Yasmine belonged to. He could picture her driving the car—too fast as usual—with her hair blowing in the wind and her favorite music blasting. She was always carefree and bubbly, which he'd admired about her. She enjoyed life and had taught him to do the same.

He didn't know much about her life now except that she was an adjunct professor at Atlanta Memorial University and also did educational consulting for the school systems in Atlanta. Doug said she'd taken a sabbatical to move back to Memphis temporarily to be with her mother.

Inhaling, Cannon opened the glass door to the wedding coordinator's office. A receptionist greeted him and instructed that he go to the waiting room, which was through the door on his right.

As he entered, he was greeted by soft wedding music playing through speakers on the wall and a familiar fragrance. He knew it instantly. It was Amarige, Yasmine's favorite perfume. Mixed with her ambrosia scent, it was always an aphrodisiac for him. No one else was in the room except him and the beauty with her head in "Modern Bride" and so engrossed in whatever she was reading, she hadn't noticed him.

His heart almost leapt out of his chest and onto the magazine-filled coffee table in front of her. She was a vision of loveliness, and he had a moment of déjà vu. When he'd met her fourteen years ago, she was reading a book to her first graders, not realizing he stood in the back of her classroom mesmerized by the sweetest voice he'd ever heard and her soft, angelic face. When she was alerted to his presence, she'd treated him to her simply amazing smile, and he knew he had to make her all his.

It wasn't the first time he'd actually met her. She'd been the geeky freshman daughter to his biology teacher when he was a senior in high school. Cannon was always cordial and spoke to Yasmine in the hallway. She wasn't on his radar, but it was something about her he'd found adorable and intriguing. However, the day he arrived to read to her students for a read-a-thon his fraternity sponsored, he definitely noticed the young, sexy teacher.

Cannon let his eyes wander over her and soak in her essence as he'd done that day in her classroom. Her hair was shorter than he remembered, but still with natural curls, and pulled back with a black head band. As always, she wore little make-up, and he noticed a few new laugh lines as she smirked over what she read. His gaze landed on her pouty lips that he'd spent endless hours kissing and nibbling as she sighed his name the entire time. Over the years, he imagined her lips on his or roaming over other parts of his body with her tongue licking and taunting him as if he were the most delectable dessert she'd ever had.

Yasmine had been his everything. His lover. His best friend. His rock. The one person he could depend on to keep him focused. She believed in him and supported his goals to the fullest. Throughout the years, he had replayed their last conversation—well, argument—in his head, trying to figure out how he could've steered it in another direction. However, he knew it would have ended the same. He hated to admit that everything was moving too fast for him, and deep down wasn't mentally ready to get married, but he never wanted to be without her.

As he stood there, he was hit by an overpowering urge to draw her into his embrace and kiss her intensely and ferociously until she couldn't think straight.

He cleared his throat, and her head rose. Their eyes locked, and the smile she had worn faded and was replaced with a questioning scowl.

"Hello, Yasmine." His voice was steady; although, if looks could kill he'd be dead.

"What the hell are you doing here?"

Okay, so maybe this isn't déjà vu.

CHAPTER TWO

When Yasmine heard her name from the familiar deep voice from the past, she thought she was dreaming, for in her dreams was the only place she experienced it. Her heart thumped against her chest as if it was ready to jump out, and the simple task of breathing was the hardest thing she'd ever done. Cannon Arrington stood less than twenty feet away from her, even more handsome and debonair than she remembered. Feelings she'd buried crept into her heart and mind, overwhelming her. Part of her wanted to run, and another part wanted to curse him out. But her aching heart wanted to fly into his warm embrace and exhale from all of the years she'd spent without him.

Instead, she stayed glued to the chair as her eyes roamed over him. His black trench coat was opened, exposing a blue suit that fit his in-shape six foot one frame as if it were made especially for him. His clean-shaven face was more chiseled and defined. Gone were his boyish grin and innocent features. He was all man now. His captivating presence in the small room reeked of importance and respect.

Yasmine told herself if she ever saw him again, she would be cordial. What happened twelve years ago was in the past, even though he'd hurt her more than she could have ever imagined. She'd managed to avoid seeing him by not coming home to Memphis often. Instead, she would give her mother an excuse as to why she should come to Atlanta or suggest they take a vacation together.

Nonetheless, there he stood, holding her eyes in a trance with his. Her skin was flushed and nausea overtook her as he casually strode over wearing that damn delicious smile as if they saw each other every day. Yasmine mustered up all the strength she had left in her as he suavely approached. She hoped she could keep her voice steady. Hoped he wouldn't realize she'd never fully gotten over him.

"I asked you a question." She was surprised her voice didn't crack, but she wasn't going to allow him to see her sweat.

"I'm here to meet with the wedding coordinator," he answered matter-of-factly.

Cannon's voice was deeper, *sexier*—sending goose bumps trailing down her arm. His woodsy aroma caught in her nose, reminding her of the times when his scent was intertwined with hers as they made love.

"But why? Doug's brother is supposed to meet me here. He's the best man."

"Change of plans. I'm the best man now."

Before she could protest, the door opened and the receptionist stuck her head in.

"Ms. Jackson is ready. I'll show you to the conference room."

Yasmine grabbed her belongings as frustration deepened in her.

Why on earth is he the best man all of a sudden, and why didn't Sherika call to tell me?

"After you, Yasmine," Cannon said, stepping back so she could walk in front of him.

A heat wave washed over her as he said her name in a sexy, seductive tone. She found herself being extra conscious of her appearance as he walked behind her. A winter white sheath dress, which stopped at her knees with a black belt wrapped around her waist, accentuating her curvy hips. Her mother had joked that morning about how sexy she looked and was she trying to score a man. Now, as Cannon cleared his throat a few times along their walk, Yasmine wondered did he think the same as her mother.

Moments later, they were settled across from each other at the conference table, with Ms. Jackson at the head going over the information for the wedding, but Yasmine couldn't concentrate. Even though she was looking at Ms. Jackson, she could feel Cannon's eyes on her, causing heat to ignite over her skin.

"So, is that okay with you?" Yasmine heard the coordinator say, but wasn't sure what it was in reference to.

"What?" Yasmine snapped out of her daze as she glanced back and forth from Cannon to Ms. Jackson.

Cannon, who could apparently listen and stare at her at the same time, chimed in.

"Can you do the cake tasting Friday afternoon?"

"Oh, sure," Yasmine said, trying to focus her attention on Ms. Jackson, but Cannon's eyes wouldn't leave her face. She crossed and uncrossed her legs as warmth shocked her womanly center. "Sherika likes amaretto and vanilla flavors, so I have an idea of what she would like."

"Perfect." Ms. Jackson flashed a smile and scratched something off of her to do list. "I forwarded the picture of the cake the bride emailed me to the bakery …"

Yasmine tuned out once again as Cannon's eyes trailed along her face and neck. She swore she could feel the heat from his breath on her skin, and she reached for the bottle of sparkling water the receptionist brought in earlier. She decided to tune back into the conversation when Ms. Jackson mentioned the music.

"I'll contact the wedding bands I usually use to see if they're available for that day. The bride said as long as they can play "Ribbon in the Sky" for their first dance, they're hired."

Yasmine's heart sank at the mention of the song. It was the song he had chosen for their wedding, and she couldn't stand to listen to it. She glanced at Cannon, who had flinched. His Adam's apple bobbed, and his eyes locked with hers as she tried to hold back the tears. Placing her notepad into her purse, she fished for her keys. She needed to escape now.

"Anything else?" Yasmine's voice croaked as she cleared her throat and took one more swig of the water. Her mouth had turned to cotton.

Ms. Jackson closed her laptop and scooted her chair back. "Nope, I think we've covered everything for now. You two just let me know your progress, and I'll do the same."

Moments later, Yasmine high-tailed it out of the office building toward the parking lot with Cannon behind her. When she stepped outside, the cold air greeted her and she realized her coat was draped over her arm, but she didn't care. She needed to get to the car. She needed to get away from him.

"Yasmine ... wait."

She hit the unlock button on her key remote. "I have to go." She opened the driver's door of her Lexus, but Cannon pushed it shut.

"Not until you look at me." His voice caressed over her like silk as he stood behind her with his hand still on top of the car.

Taking a deep breath, she turned to face him. Her breathing stifled as she looked up at his handsome face. It took everything she had not to run her hand along his strong jawline up to his hair and twirl a finger around a curl.

"What?"

"I know this has to be uncomfortable for you, but I just hope we'll be able to work together to make Sherika and Doug's special day perfect."

"I don't see that as a problem considering there really isn't a need to see or speak to you again until the wedding weekend."

"Um … no. I'll see you this Friday at the cake tasting."

"Wait? What? Why do you have to be there? I'm just sampling cakes for the bridal cake."

"But Doug wants a groom's cake, so I told him I would take care of that. Weren't you listening to the conversation earlier?" he asked with a smirk and a raised eyebrow.

Of course she wasn't paying attention to the conversation. She was too busy trying to pretend to listen as Cannon stared her down like a tiger ready to pounce on his prey.

"I … must've misunderstood."

"How's your mother?"

"Fine." She wanted to keep her answers short. The less he knew about her life the better.

"I was disappointed to learn she has cancer," he said with sincerity in his voice. "Please give her my best."

"She's in remission and doing a lot better." Yasmine tried to avoid eye contact with him, but it was hard since he overpowered her personal space. Plus, she was pinned against the car and his hand was still on top of it over her shoulder.

"How long will you be in Memphis?"

"Until the beginning of summer."

"Maybe we can have dinner. Go over the wedding plans and catch up."

"I can't," she said in a strained voice.

His hand slid off of the car, brushing her shoulder and down her bare arm in the process. Yasmine winced at his subtle, warm touch. They stared at each other in silence, and she was scared of what he may do or say, especially when he stepped toward her, closing what little space was between them. His sexy mouth was just inches from hers, and she yearned to kiss him to know what heaven felt like again.

"Well, if you change your mind." He paused, brushing a curl off her forehead that had fallen out of her headband on her brisk walk to the car. "Call me. My contact information is in the packet the coordinator gave you."

Stepping back, he turned to open the car door for her. Without acknowledging him, she slid into the car, tossing her coat and purse onto the passenger seat. She reached to close the door, but he shut it for her and stood outside for a second, staring at her through the tinted window before walking away. Tears burned her eyes, but she was too mad to let them roll down her face.

She started the car, turned on her cell phone, and noticed she had several missed calls and voicemails from Sherika. Yasmine had forgotten to turn her cell phone back on after a meeting with a group of elementary school principals.

She activated the hands free system to call Sherika. She had some explaining to do. Yasmine pulled out of the parking lot as the phone rang through the speakers.

"Yasmine. I'm so glad you finally called me back. I've been—"

"Why on earth is Cannon suddenly the best man?"

"Calm down. I didn't know until right before the meeting either. Doug had been trying to call me, but my third graders did a mock test this morning to prepare for the upcoming standardized test, so you know cell phones can't be on."

"I don't know if I can …" She tried to hold back the tears, but it was no use. One streamed down her face followed by another, and she wiped them way before they clouded her vision as she drove.

"You can't back out! You're my best friend."

Yasmine could hear the urgency and panic in her friend's voice, and she felt bad. She couldn't be selfish, but planning a wedding with Cannon wasn't exactly on her bucket list.

"It took everything I had not to slap him … or worse, kiss him."

"Girl, I know he hurt you, but please try to suck it up for me. I need you."

Yasmine sighed as she turned onto the interstate. They'd been best friends since fifth grade when Sherika moved to Memphis from Gary, Indiana. They went to middle and high school together, as well as Tennessee State University, pledged the same sorority, taught together in Nashville and then New York until Yasmine moved to Atlanta a few years ago to finish her doctorate. Both only children, they were more like sisters, and Yasmine knew she couldn't disappoint her best friend.

"If you weren't my girl …"

Sherika let out a big sigh. "Oh thank goodness, and I promise there really isn't much you have to do with him."

"If you say so. I have a cake tasting appointment on Friday afternoon, and he'll be there to sample the groom's cakes."

"I'm kinda glad you'll be there at the same time. Doug just wants plain chocolate, nothing fancy. But perhaps you could find a chocolate with a little more kick. I spoke to the baker, and she said she'll have about six to eight chocolate samples to select from, so make sure it's not just plain chocolate."

"Yes, bridezilla." Yasmine laughed. "I'm just teasing."

"Girl, by the end of this you won't be teasing. I hate not being there, but I'm so glad Doug and I have friends like you and Cannon to help make our special day perfect."

Yasmine cringed at his name and hated being reminded he would be helping. However, Sherika was her friend, and her peace of mind during the planning of the wedding was more important.

"I'm not going to let you down."

Yasmine walked into Ollie's Sweets at exactly two o'clock to find Cannon already there chatting with Ollie Moss, the owner and head baker. Sherika and Yasmine used to frequent the downtown Memphis bakery as teenagers, and she wasn't surprised to learn that the bride-to-be had selected their favorite bakery to make the wedding cakes.

"Hi, Ms. Ollie."

"Look at my Yaz all grown up." The ladies hugged and Yasmine inhaled Ms. Ollie's fragrance. She always smelled like vanilla and buttercream icing. Stepping back, she got a good look at Ms. Ollie. She still had the same sweet smile and grandmother nature that always made customers feel at home in her bakery.

"Hello, Yasmine," Cannon's deep voice stated behind her.

She turned and nodded to acknowledge his presence. Staring up at him, she tried to stifle a gulp or two as her heartbeat sped up. He was dressed casually in khakis and a light blue sweater that fit his sexy physique. Cannon had never been overly muscular, but he'd always been in shape, and the way his sweater fit over his arms and abs suggested he still worked out.

His fresh scent loomed into her personal space, outweighing the aroma of all the cakes and pastries in the bakery. She wasn't sure how long she could do this, but she'd made a promise to her best friend.

"Well, let's get started," Ms. Ollie stated. "Follow me. I have everything set up in the tasting room."

Yasmine flinched as Cannon placed his warm hand at the small of her back, causing a flow of burning desire to rush through her veins. She cleared her throat and walked faster to escape his touch searing her skin. As his hand fell, it brushed against her butt, and she gave him a glare. He mouthed "sorry" and placed his hands mischievously in his pocket. She knew it was probably an accident but wasn't sure how sorry he was about doing it. He'd always known just the right way to caress and kiss her body, and no other man had turned her on as much as he had.

When they entered the tasting room, there was a long table laden with dessert plates of miniature cupcakes. On small pink cards, the flavor of the cupcake was written in calligraphy. Yasmine snapped a few pictures with her digital camera to email to Sherika for her wedding memory book.

"There are six mini cupcakes of each cake flavor that I discussed with the bride and groom for you to sample. On the bistro table," Ms. Ollie paused as she pointed to a small table by the window, "you'll find a list of the flavors for you to take notes and to check off the ones you like. The bride wants three different flavors since her cake has three layers, and for the groom's cake two different flavors of chocolate. There's also bottled water. I suggest you take a few sips to clean your palate before trying a different flavor. If you need anything, I'll be next door working on a cake for a wedding tomorrow, but will be in and out to check on you."

After she left, Yasmine placed her coat and purse on a chair at the bistro table and Cannon immediately went to the cupcakes.

"Which should we try first?" he asked.

He handed her an empty dessert plate as his eyes roamed over her black cropped sweater that stopped at the belt of her dark skinny jeans, down to her black knee-high boots before rising back up to settle on her face which she knew had to be flushed because her cheeks were burning. She placed her focus on the tasty cupcakes to avoid looking in his direction.

"Can't decide. They all look delicious, but I know Sherika loves amaretto so let's try that one and one of the chocolates for the groom's cake," Yasmine answered with ease, and was surprised she wasn't as nervous being alone with him as she thought she would be, despite the way he'd just raked his eyes over her like an x-ray.

She grabbed the two amaretto cupcakes while Cannon grabbed two German chocolates, and they settled in at the table.

"Did you eat something before coming?" he asked, taking a sip of the water.

"Not since breakfast." She sipped her water. "What about you?"

"The same. You know I love eating anything sweet and couldn't wait to get here." He had a sparkle in his eye and a wicked grin crossed his face.

Yasmine blinked her eyes a few times at his comment. Cannon had a way of saying something normal, but there was always a sexual connotation behind it. She thought surely she'd heard emphasis on the word eating. Her mind transported her to a time where he'd done just that while they were at his parent's home visiting for the weekend, and he told her not to make a sound. Starting from her forehead, he'd kissed and licked every inch of her, enticing her breasts in his warm mouth, before lingering in the sensitive area between her legs longer than the other places until he drove her crazy with an unruly, muffled orgasm. She squirmed in her chair at the memory.

"Are you ready to begin?" he asked picking up the chocolate cupcake.

She snapped out of the daydream she'd had plenty times before. "Yep." She picked up the amaretto one. "Bon appétit."

She bit into her cupcake while Cannon popped the entire thing into his mouth, leaving a little bit of chocolate icing on the corner of his bottom lip. Yasmine's eyes settled on the delectable spot. She wanted nothing more than to reach across the table and lick the chocolate off of him and taste his lips that she'd missed so much.

"Mmm … that was good," he said and proceeded to swish his tongue to the side where the icing lay. "You have to try this one."

I wanted to, but you beat me to it.

For the next twenty minutes they sampled cupcakes and compared notes. Yasmine was trying to keep the conversation only to the task at hand, and so far it worked. She found herself a little more at ease with him. She wasn't sure what to expect, but he'd been a gentleman, which was his nature.

"How many more do we have?" she asked, taking a sip of water as Cannon stood at the table grabbing two more cupcakes and setting them on the bistro table in front of her.

"This is the last chocolate one for the groom's cake and there are two more to taste for the bride's cake. Think you can hang?"

Yasmine laughed and patted her stomach. "I think so. I'm actually ready for some real food now."

"Me too. I guess we ate dessert first." He laughed and took a bite of the cake. "This chocolate mint flavor is good. I think we have a winner."

She bit into hers. "You're right. This really is good. Let's make it the second layer for the groom's cake," she suggested, remembering what Sherika said about having a different flavor besides plain chocolate.

"Sounds good to me." He checked it off on his list and pushed the plate aside, resting his arms crossed in front of him on the table and leaning toward her. "Never been much of a chocolate fan. I prefer caramel."

Yasmine almost choked on her cupcake and lifted her head to meet his smoldering gaze. There was no laughter in his words or on his face. Instead, she noted the seriousness in his tone and the way his eyes examined her as if he was reading her mind and liked what he read.

"How's everything?"

Cannon and Yasmine both jumped at the words as Ms. Ollie entered the room. Yasmine was glad for the interruption. The way Cannon had moved toward her she thought he was going to kiss her, and considering where her thoughts had just returned, she would've let him.

Cannon relaxed back into his chair and patted his midsection. "Perfect," he answered with a smile and Yasmine was glad that he had. She was still in a daze.

"Good." Ms. Ollie glanced at the cake table. "I see you have a few more to sample. I'll be back in about twenty minutes to go over any questions you may have and pack up the uneaten cupcakes for you."

The smile he'd displayed for Ms. Ollie vanished when she left and was once more replaced with a serious facade. Yasmine knew all of his facial expressions, and this one was screaming she needed to move and move fast before he reached for her like he had the first time they'd made love.

"Cannon …"

"Yes, Yasmine?" His voice was deep. Provocative. Stimulating. She needed to escape, but his eyes held hers in a deep hypnotic trance that she couldn't break.

"We need to finish the last two samples for the bridal cake," she managed to stammer out, wanting to tear her eyes away from his but couldn't.

"Are you sure that's what you want to do?" He leaned in closer as she scooted her chair away from the table. He raised his eyebrow. "Your expression isn't saying that. I know you *very* well, or have you forgotten?"

"You don't know me."

"I know every single inch of you." His baritone voice was serious and sexy.

Sensations blazed through each cell of her body, for in her heart she knew he was speaking the truth. He would spend hours exploring her body with his fingers, tongue, and lips, driving her completely insane.

"I know that spot on the back of your neck that takes you past the point of no return. There's a special way I would kiss and nibble that area. I do believe it's about an inch below your hair line. I used to love when we would go out, and I would sit next to you, gliding my fingers along your neck and watching you maintain your composure. Of course you never could, and we would end up making love in the car or you would pleasure me all the way home. Thank goodness my Mustang had tinted windows. I would've hated for some perv to see your head in my lap. We could barely get in the door and ended up making love right on the foyer floor. Or those three beauty marks on your outer left thigh. I remember them quite well, as my tongue would pass them on my way down…"

"Cannon ..." she whispered as her memory took her back to those times. She quickly went to the dessert table to hide her face, which she was sure was bright red.

His damn spot. She had told other guys about the hot spot, but none of them sent the same electrifying volts through her like he had. It was as if Cannon's name was invisibly tattooed on the back of her neck, and the other guys knew it was there and could not perform under such high expectations. It would immediately turn her off, so after a while she stopped mentioning it. Instead, when men would ask where her spot was located, she would tell them to go find it. But they never did. Every inch of her body was programmed to Cannon's touch.

"You know I can go on and on," he said in her ear, his lips brushing over it as he spoke; his hands holding onto her hips with his chest meshed against her back. The familiar warmth and scent of him radiated onto her skin. For a moment, she wanted to be surrounded by his presence and comforted for having to be without him for so long. But then reality sunk in, and she remembered that this was the only man who had ever broken her heart and getting back into her life wasn't going to be easy.

"I'd rather you not." She moved down to the uneaten cupcakes before she did something she would regret, like turning around and kissing him. "This isn't the time or place. Ms. Ollie will be back soon."

"Let's have dinner after we leave here. You said earlier you were hungry."

"All of this sampling has made me full." She picked up a plate, but he took it from her and slammed it on the table. She was surprised it didn't break.

"Yasmine, I know you're trying to avoid me, but that's going to be impossible considering we've been commissioned to help plan a wedding for our best friends."

"The next assignment on my list is the bridesmaid's dresses, and I totally doubt you'll be wearing a dress, unless there's something you forgot to tell me." She raised an eyebrow.

"The only thing I know about dresses is unzipping or raising them up to get under them, as you very well know." His eyes were heated with a sexual stare that she knew all too well.

"Can we please get through the cake tasting without traveling down memory lane?"

"Yaz, I just thought we could—"

"We could what? Catch up? Shoot the breeze? Be friends?" She laughed sarcastically.

"Honestly, yes." He stood in her personal space, and she stepped back finding herself against the wall next to the dessert table.

"Look, Dr. Arrington. Don't think for a minute you can just waltz back into my life and think everything is cool between us because it's not! You ..." She stopped as the tears stung her eyes. She wanted to flee as one tear glided down her cheek. *Darn it!*

Cannon stepped closer and wiped it with his finger, causing another one to take its place.

He placed his hands tenderly on either side of her face and locked his eyes with hers. "I've never missed anyone as much as I have missed you."

CHAPTER THREE

Cannon stared down at the hurt woman in front of him. He'd hated the way their relationship ended. She'd been fed up with his workaholic ways for too long. Yasmine's father had been a workaholic who died when she was ten years old, and Cannon knew that had always bothered her. She always tried to get him to slow down and relax out of the fear he would face the same fate as her father. While she'd understood he was in medical school, she hated when he placed other projects before her. There were times when he'd been late or cancelled dates and trips because of his dedication to extracurricular activities and not knowing how to say no to people. His father had taught him at a young age to be chivalrous and an active member of the community. What Cannon hadn't learned was how to pay attention to his woman. He'd taken her for granted and had a rude awakening when she was no longer in his life.

After Yasmine called off their engagement, he'd never heard from her again despite his attempts to call her before he left for Brazil. Unfortunately, all of his calls, doorbell ringing, emails and letters had gone unanswered. The only time he'd heard from her was when she'd mailed back an uncashed check he'd sent to cover the cost of cancellations for the places she had reserved for their wedding. It came back torn up with a note that read, "Please stop contacting me." When he returned from Brazil a year later, he learned from Doug that she had moved to New York along with Sherika to teach at a private school.

Cannon wasn't sure what to expect when they saw each other again. If they couldn't be friends, he thought they could at least be cordial for the sake of planning their friend's wedding. However, it had never dawned on him just how much he'd hurt her. Now, staring at her with silent tears staining her soft cheeks and her sexy quivering lips, he knew, and he hated that even more.

"I hurt you," he said, sighing softly. "And I've felt guilty about that every single day we've been apart."

She stared up at him with her heartbreaking eyes before looking away, shaking her head.

"I don't want to discuss this. Besides, Ms. Ollie will be back soon." She tried to move, but he encircled his arms around her waist, holding her firm against him.

"Yasmine ... there is so much I need to say to you, which is one reason I would like to see you outside of the wedding planning so we can talk. We need to talk."

"There really isn't a need to. You're my past, and I wish to keep you there." She squirmed out of his embrace and placed a few feet of distance between them. "Besides, I don't care about anything you have to say or how guilty you feel for hurting me. And I can't believe you missed me. Puleeze. It's obvious you didn't want to marry me or you wouldn't have ..." Her voice trailed off. As she turned away from him, he grabbed her to him once more, this time holding her tighter against him.

"That's not true, and you know it," he stated through clenched teeth. "I never said I didn't want to marry you. I just wasn't ready at that particular time."

"Exactly, because you had your *once in a lifetime opportunity* to pursue, which was more important than being with me."

"I never said that."

She managed to push him away, and he was quite surprised at her strength, but she was angry.

"I was young and naïve and thought my world revolved around you. Whatever you did, I supported you and placed my dreams on the backburner. When you were accepted to John Hopkins and asked me to marry you, I was in the process of applying to graduate schools. I received an acceptance letter to Vanderbilt a few weeks after we were engaged, but by then we were in the process of planning our wedding and making plans to move to Baltimore in the fall. So then I started researching grad schools in the Baltimore and Washington, DC area and that's when you changed our plans."

"Why didn't you tell me about Vanderbilt or that you wanted to obtain your master's degree?"

"Because during that time you were stressed with rounds at the hospital and waiting to hear back about the grant as well as the residency programs you applied for."

"Yasmine, I—"

"Oh just shut up! I don't want to hear anything you have to say. I didn't want to hear it then, and I don't want to hear it now. You've missed me? Well guess what? You *had* me. I was all yours."

She turned away from him, grabbed the last cupcake to sample, and headed back to the bistro table fuming. "Ms. Ollie will be back soon, and we aren't done."

"This conversation isn't over with yet," he said, rejoining her at the table. "We still need to talk."

"No we don't. I just want to get through this process and go back to my life without you in it.

However, I promised my best friend she would have the best wedding ever, so if that means having to be in contact with you during this planning process, I can agree to be cordial but nothing more."

"I can respect that."

He wasn't sure if he was telling the truth or not, for there was more he needed to get off his chest just as she had done, but this wasn't the time or place. Seeing her again reminded him even more how much he'd missed her. How much he needed her back in his life. He knew in his heart he would always love her, but being in her presence confirmed he was still in love with her.

Ms. Ollie entered moments later and Cannon and Yasmine gave her their choices for the cakes. After saying their good-byes, they walked in silence to the parking lot. Cannon was trying to search for the right words to say without messing up their agreement on being cordial. Yasmine did seem to be in a pleasant mood while Ms. Ollie packed up the mini cupcakes. He knew it wouldn't happen overnight, but Yasmine had always been the only one for him, and he planned on getting her back.

As they approached her car, he was hesitant in saying good-bye. She'd turned him down for dinner, and he didn't want to push her away. She needed time to get used to him being in her life again. As she unlocked the door, her phone began to ring with Brandy's song "Best Friend."

"What's up, girl?"

Cannon opened the door for her as she leaned over, tossing her purse and the bakery bag in the passenger seat. His eyes settled on her butt sitting tight and firm in her jeans. She was more curvy now, with hips that he wanted to grab and lift up on him or push her into the car and kiss her senseless as he had on their first date. He couldn't get enough of her sexy lips that night as she sighed breathlessly in his arms, running her hands through his hair and down his face. His manhood stiffened at the memory.

"Really? Goodness, that's a lot of money, girl." She continued with "uh huh's" as she listened to who he assumed was Sherika.

"Okay, I'll see what I can do. Don't worry about anything."

"What's wrong?" he asked when Yasmine pressed the end button on her smart phone.

"That was Sherika. The wedding coordinator sent her the estimate for the flower arrangements, and it was outrageous. She's going to email a copy to me so I can figure out how to cut the cost before Sherika signs with this particular florist."

"Would you mind forwarding the invoice to me? I know of some florists that may be less but still do beautiful work."

She cocked her head to the side with a puzzled expression. "Sure. I'll do it when I get home."

"What?" He shrugged. "I like to help out, you know that. Trust me, I know nothing about floral arrangements." And he didn't, but anything to stay in contact with her, because at this point the rest of their assignments didn't involve each other.

She slid into the car. "Okay. Will do."

"Thank you," he said as he closed her door with a smile.

Yasmine sat on her bed with her laptop going over a presentation for next week, but her thoughts kept traveling to Cannon. She hated that she'd let him get so close to her, and now his scent was embedded on her skin, tormenting her sanity. She hated the way he'd held her in his arms as if she belonged there, and now she longed to feel them around her once more.

She hated he saw the tears on her cheeks, but wanted so desperately to lay her head on his chest and cry her eyes out for being without him for so long.

She'd never stopped loving him. Instead, she learned how to live without him.

Yasmine fell for him when she was a geeky freshman in high school and he was a senior. Class president, president of the Academic and Science Clubs, as well as captain of the golf team, he was one of the most popular and handsome boys at their school. Besides nodding his head and saying hello in the hallway, he barely knew she was alive. The only reason he acknowledged her was because her mother was his mentor and favorite teacher. Eight years later, when Yasmine was reading to her first grade class waiting for the volunteer reader, she was pleasantly surprised to see Cannon Arrington standing in the doorway, staring at her as if she was the most beautiful woman in the world. That had been fourteen years ago, and he still stirred her heart as he had then.

The less she saw or spoke to him the better because she didn't want to fall for him again. But she knew in her heart that would be impossible. Cannon had a charismatic air about him that drew her to him, and she didn't know how much longer she could handle planning the wedding if it meant having to deal with him.

She closed her laptop, grabbed her cell phone, and went to the kitchen for a slice of leftover pizza. She was alone tonight in the house she grew up in. Her mother was spending the weekend out of town with her boyfriend. Yasmine was happy that her mother found love again after losing her husband. Frederick Dubose had been a workaholic, working around the clock as a financial analyst. He died from his second heart attack on Christmas Eve when Yasmine was only ten. She'd been devastated because she was a daddy's girl. While dating Cannon, she realized how similar he was to her father, and she tried to make him stop and smell the roses every once and a while, but that didn't last long. She wasn't surprised when he wanted to postpone their wedding, considering he'd postponed or cancelled everything else, which was why she felt the best thing to do was to let him go. He'd hurt her too many times and that was the last straw.

The ringing of her cell phone startled her. Glancing at the clock on the stove, she saw it was almost midnight. It was a Memphis number she didn't recognize but answered it anyway.

"Hello?" she asked in a cautious manner.

"Hey there," the sexy, deep voice on the other end answered.

Her heart dropped. Why was Cannon calling her so late … or at all?

"I wanted to talk to you about the floral arrangements. I figured you'd still be awake."

"I was just about to turn in so make it quick," she said in a curt tone and immediately felt bad about it. This wasn't about them. It was about making sure her best friend had the wedding of her dreams.

"I spoke to my brother-in-law's cousin who is the event planner for his restaurant. She also does floral arrangements on the side. I sent her the invoice, and she can do the same arrangements for half or maybe even a third of the cost by ordering the flowers wholesale from a distributor she uses."

"Really? That would be great, but have you seen her work?"

"Yes. She did the floral arrangements for Shelbi and Bria's weddings. They were out of this world. Better than the ones that the wedding coordinator showed us."

She placed the slice of pizza in the microwave and hit one minute. "Wait. I knew Bria was married because I saw her all over magazines and the Internet with ex basketball player Rasheed Vincent, but when did little Shelbi get married?" She'd also seen pictures of the wedding party, including one with Cannon looking suave and handsome in his tuxedo.

He laughed. "Little Shelbi is all grown up now. She got married a year ago to Justin Richardson. He's the owner and chef of Lillian's Dinner and Blues Club over on Beale. She's also in her second year of her residency at Memphis Central."

"That's great. I thought she would be a chef at her own restaurant. Your baby sister can cook."

"She still can, but she leaves it to her husband now. But she did have a short stint as a food critic, and she has a food blog called "Cooking up Love." However, my parents were happy when she decided to continue her medical career instead."

"I know your parents wanted you all to become doctors. How are they doing?"

"They're quite well and semi-retired, working only three days a week even though my father is still a heart surgeon so he may work more days at the hospital. They travel a lot. Raven and I run the practice now."

"How's Raven? Is she married with children? That's all she talked about."

"Well, she did get married a few years ago, but her husband was a police officer and died in the line of duty three months after their wedding."

"That's horrible. I'm truly sorry to hear that. How is she coping?"

"Well, you know Raven. She knows how to be strong on the outside, but as her twin brother, I know it still hurts her. I think she needs a change of scenery."

"Wow. A lot has changed in twelve years."

"Yes it has, and I would love to continue to catch up with you, Yaz," he said in a sincere manner. "I meant what I said earlier. I've missed you."

"Cannon—"

"I know. I won't say anything else. However, Zaria, that's Justin cousin, can meet with us tomorrow afternoon at the restaurant if you're free to look at her portfolio."

Yasmine was glad for the change of subject. She could feel herself wanting to tell him just how much she'd missed him, too.

"Yes. The sooner the better. Sherika called me earlier frustrated about something else. Luckily she and Doug will be here in a few weeks to meet with the coordinator and the caterer."

"That's good. There's only so much we can do considering it's not our wedding."

She sighed. It was time to get off the phone before she said the wrong thing.

"What time?"

"Zaria said around four. Do you need me to pick you up?"

"No, I know where Beale Street is. I'm sure I can find the restaurant."

"Just checking. I'll be on your side of town tomorrow. I'm going to beat Sean in a round a golf since the weather is going to be nice."

"How could I forget about Sean? How is he?"

"The same. Still a player. He says he's a lifelong bachelor, but he just needs a good woman to make him fall."

"I'm sure he'll meet the right woman one day." She let out a big yawn. "Sorry. It's been a long day." *More like a long week.*

"Well ... I'll let you get some rest."

She could hear the reluctance in his voice, but she knew it was time to get off the phone. When they'd first started dating, they would talk on the phone all night, and she didn't want this to be one of those sessions.

"All right, see you tomorrow."
"Sweet dreams, Yasmine."

CHAPTER FOUR

Yasmine sat in her car in the parking lot behind Lillian's and took a deep breath. She was frustrated by the fact that she had to see Cannon again for the third time in a week. She almost ran her fingers through her hair, but stopped as she remembered she'd just left the salon and didn't want to mess it up. Her hair was styled in the pixie cut that she normally wore, but since she'd been back in Memphis, she just washed her hair and wore her natural curls.

She'd tossed and turned the night before after getting off of the phone with him. His voice in her ear had turned her on. She found herself as she had many nights before pretending her hands were his, running them over her body as he would, caressing her breasts tenderly and then moving down to her moist center, massaging herself with an urgency of needing to feel him inside of her again, driving her crazy as always. She screamed his name when her orgasm erupted through her body sending her into convulsions. His scent, which still lingered on her from earlier, seeped through her pores and mingled with her sweat that had drenched her body and sheets. She smiled briefly before the tears began to flow. She missed the way their bodies would be meshed together, wet and uninhibited. The few men she'd been with after him could never carry her to a place of serenity and complete freedom as he had. With him she could be herself sexually and sensually, holding nothing back. After one more round of pleasure, she'd finally managed to drift off to sleep, not completely satisfied because he was the only one that could accomplish that.

Now she had to face him once again and hoped that last night's guilty pleasure wasn't written all over her face. A black BMW sedan backed into the parking space beside her, and the driver's window rolled down. She pushed the button to do the same on her car.

"Been waiting long?" Cannon asked.

"Nope. Just pulled up a few minutes ago."

Moments later they walked to the front of the restaurant. Cannon was on his cell phone with Zaria asking her to unlock the door because the restaurant didn't open until five. Yasmine walked slightly behind him taking in the view. He was dressed in a pair of khakis that hugged his butt perfectly, a gold golf shirt with an argyle black and gold sweater vest over it. His invigorating scent turned her on even more, and she hoped she wouldn't jump him as last night's escapade still invaded her thoughts.

When they approached the door, a handsome man in a chef's jacket and untamed, curly sexy hair leaned against the door.

"What's up, Justin?" Cannon asked. "I was expecting to see Zaria."

"I'm waiting for Shelbi."

Cannon turned to Yasmine and made introductions.

They shook hands, and she could definitely see Shelbi with Justin. He was the cool, artsy type that Shelbi used to hang with when she was a teenager.

"Nice to meet you, Yasmine," Justin said and glanced at Cannon. "Are you two staying for dinner?

We have a band playing tonight that mixes R&B with jazz and blues. You have to check it out."

"I don't know." Cannon turned to Yasmine with a raised eyebrow and a sly smile. "Are we staying for dinner?"

Yasmine hated being put on the spot, especially considering Justin seemed sincere and excited about them eating at his establishment. However, she refused to let Cannon get his way. She agreed to be cordial but not accommodating.

"That sounds really nice, Justin, but I can't tonight. However, I'll come back with my mother before I move back to Atlanta."

"Cool. Let me know in advance so you can sit in the VIP section."

They bid Justin good-bye as he stayed outside to wait for his wife.

"What was that about?" Yasmine asked as they stood alone in the dining room. "You didn't have to put me on the spot just to get me to have dinner with you."

"I wasn't trying to. He asked, not me ... but I think you'd like Lillian's. It reminds me of the place I took you for our first date."

Yasmine had been so angry with him that she hadn't noticed the restaurant. It wasn't some hole in the wall juke joint; it was a very classy establishment. Red brocade toppers adorned black tablecloths under glass overlays and silverware rolled in black napkins. Wineglasses and a candle in the middle elegantly finished the inviting table scene. The walnut hardwood floors shone brilliantly, and brick walls rose two stories, ornamented with abstract pieces. There was another dining area on the second floor and sparkling chandeliers were strategically placed throughout the entire restaurant adding to its stylish ambiance. She'd read the reviews online before coming and learned that it was a southern soul food restaurant that focused on healthy ways to prepare meals. She thought perhaps she could order something to go, because she didn't want to sit across a table from Cannon.

"It's quite beautiful and the aromas floating from the kitchen are making me hungry, but I'm not promising you a dinner date tonight," she said, following him through the dining area to a hallway of offices. They stopped in front of a slightly ajar door, and Cannon lightly knocked on it.

"Who said anything about a date?" He winked and pushed the door open. "Hey, Zaria."

"You're late," Zaria Richardson said in a serious tone as she stood from her desk. She was a tall, strikingly beautiful woman with smooth, toffee skin and flowing brown hair down to her waist that wasn't a weave or a wig. Her red suit fit like a glove and stopped right before her knees, showcasing long legs. She should've been on a run way in Paris not an event planner for a restaurant.

"Blame your cousin." Cannon laughed as he gave Zaria a hug. "We were here on time."

After he made the introductions, they looked over the portfolios. Yasmine was quite impressed with the bouquets and flower arrangements that Zaria had created for various functions at the restaurant, as well as weddings and receptions.

"These are exquisite," Yasmine said as she continued to flip the pages, taking note of the prices of the arrangements. Sherika would definitely be pleased.

"Have you thought about doing this full-time?" Cannon inquired.

"Well, it's funny you mentioned it. My cousin Reagan is a wedding planner in Atlanta and has asked me several times to go into business with her, so I have thought about it. We always said along with

Brooklyn's expertise in photography that we should, but it's just a dream."

"You should make that dream a reality. You're also a great event planner, and Rasheed is always bragging how his baby sister is an excellent photographer. I don't see why the three of you wouldn't have a successful company."

She laughed. "Maybe one day. So, Yasmine, let's go through the pictures on my iPad and tag the ones you think Sherika would like, and I'll email them to her."

After thirty minutes, Cannon excused himself and left the office to which Yasmine was grateful that he did. She could concentrate better with him gone. He wasn't even looking at the flowers. Instead, he sat on the couch playing on his smart phone and glancing at her with a smile. If he wasn't going to help, he didn't need to come. She could select floral arrangements without him. Then it dawned on her that he'd arranged it on purpose. After yesterday, there really wouldn't be a need to stay in contact because the rest of the tasks didn't require for them to see each other until the wedding weekend.

"So Cannon tells me you two used to be engaged when he was in medical school and now you're planning a wedding for your best friends. You must be one tough cookie. I don't think I could plan a wedding with my ex fiancé and not feel some type of animosity toward him."

Yasmine laughed. She was trying to be a tough cookie on the outside, but on the inside, she was cookie dough in a mixing bowl. She honestly didn't know how she was going to make it through the next few months. Cannon definitely wasn't going anywhere, or so it seemed, and was trying to find every reason in the book to see her. If he showed up to her dress fitting with the bridesmaids next week, she would scream.

"Well, it hasn't been easy, that's for sure, but I'm doing this for my best friend. I want her to have a beautiful day."

"That's the spirit. And who knows. Maybe this is fate. Perhaps you two were meant to be."

A light rap at the door interrupted their conversation, and she hoped it wasn't Cannon.

"Yaz!" a lady squealed as she entered the room. Yasmine turned and saw Shelbi in pink scrubs charging toward her for a hug. She looked the same overall with her shoulder length hair pulled into a bouncy pony tail and a beautiful smile that was just like Cannon's, but she was hippier than Yasmine remembered and had grown an inch or two.

"Oh my goodness, look at you," Yasmine said, hugging Shelbi tightly. She had been her favorite out of all the Arrington siblings because of her sweet personality and laid back nature. "You're all grown up."

"And you look like you're in your twenties. Are you drinking from the fountain of youth?"

"Thank you. You were always such a sweetheart. Congrats on your marriage. I met your hubby earlier. He's a cutie."

Shelbi sat down in the other chair in front of the desk next to Yasmine while Zaria started to email the pictures to Sherika.

"Thank you. Now let's change the subject," Shelbi said with wide grin. "My brother is still crazy about you."

"Whatever."

"No, seriously. I promise after y'all broke up, he wasn't the same for a while. He was moody and snappy. He's always been easy going. He sunk himself further into staying busy, and he just seemed withdrawn sometimes. When he started to date again, they weren't serious ... well, except one, but he broke up with her a few summers ago because she kept pressuring him into marrying her. I think she was trying to get pregnant on the sly."

Yasmine shrugged. "Maybe Cannon isn't the marrying kind."

"No, Sean isn't the marrying kind, but Cannon is. He just hasn't the found the one yet because he's still in love with you. Heck, I tried to hook him up with Zaria but—"

"He is not my type," Zaria said with a slight attitude looking up from her iPad.

Shelbi laughed. "I know. Besides, you have your eyes set on someone else. Yasmine, she has this love/hate relationship with Dr. Braxton, a friend of the family. He is completely smitten with Zaria, but she won't go out with him."

"Ignore Shelbi about Dr. Braxton, but seriously, listen to her about Cannon. When he called yesterday about the floral arrangements, I knew something was up. One, he never calls me and two, men don't care about floral arrangements. I've helped many a bride, and I've never met a groom until the wedding day. Besides, as soon as we started looking at the arrangements, he up and left. I glanced at my monitor, and he's in the sports bar area watching a game and drinking a beer. He just came to see you."

"Ladies, I ... don't think he's still in love with me. I just think he feels bad about how our relationship ended."

Shelbi stood. "I'm sure he does, but I know my big brother very well." She glanced at the clock on the wall. "He's ecstatic you're in town. I was only a teenager when you were together, but I admired your relationship and hoped to find true love one day, and I did."

"Well, I'm glad you found your true love. Justin seems like a sweetheart."

"He is. I gotta run back to the hospital. But since you're here, you might as well as stay for dinner. My hubby can throw down in the kitchen."

The ladies hugged one more time before Shelbi skipped out of the office.

"I'm done emailing the pictures to Sherika," Zaria said, closing her iPad case and standing with a set of keys in her hand. "Do you want me to take you to where Cannon is or are you hightailing it out the back door?"

Yasmine sighed as she stood and grabbed her purse. "I guess having dinner with Cannon isn't the end of the world."

CHAPTER FIVE

Cannon studied Yasmine over the top of his menu while she read over hers. She'd been staring at it for over five minutes. He wasn't sure if she was trying to avoid him or if she really didn't know what to order. He remembered her being somewhat of a picky eater. There were certain foods she didn't like, which included tomatoes, squash, and mushrooms.

He thought back to their first date over fourteen years ago. He'd taken her to a place similar to Lillian's. Yasmine wore a multi-colored sundress that stopped right above her knees, showcasing her sexy legs that he couldn't keep his eyes off of. All the men in the place had been staring at her, and he was proud that she was with him.

When the hostess at Lillian's had shown them to the VIP section earlier, he'd noticed a repeat. Heads turned and smiles formed in her direction from the majority of the men, but he couldn't blame them. She was fine in the winter white dress slacks that fit nice and snug over her butt. He enjoyed the view from behind as her hips swished back and forth, causing an awakening in his manhood. He was relieved when they finally reached the booth before she noticed from his khakis how much he enjoyed watching her walk. The pink, backless halter showcased her smooth back that he wanted to run his lips over, making sure to kiss the spot on her neck that drove her insane.

He continued his perusal of her as she stared at the menu. Her sexy haircut brought out her high cheek bones, and her doe-shaped eyes showed off her simply amazing smile that he'd fallen in love with at first glance. The halter blouse she wore displayed toned arms and silky, caramel skin that taunted him to run a finger over to hear her cute giggle.

Her personality hadn't changed much. She still had a pleasant, warm-hearted demeanor and very little ruffled her feathers, except maybe having to plan the wedding with him. Yasmine wasn't as bubbly as she used to be, but she had matured over the years into a very independent and intelligent woman.

Unfortunately, her brick wall guarded her, but he was determined to bulldoze it down.

Cannon closed his menu and took a sip of his white wine. "The shrimp and grits are really good, and you can ask for them without the stewed tomatoes," he suggested. "I know you love anything with shrimp."

She glanced at him for a second before placing her eyes back on the menu. "I was looking at that along with a salad." Closing her menu, she placed it on top of his. "What are you ordering?"

"The oven-fried chicken with the organic collards."

"I read a lot of great reviews about this place, and I can't believe he really doesn't serve pork in Memphis of all places."

"Nope. I get my ribs from Rendezvous."

"Love Rendezvous. Growing up, my dad would take us there once a month. They have the best barbeque. I'll have to make sure to go by there before I go back to Atlanta."

Their conversation was interrupted briefly by the waitress who took their order and mentioned the band would be playing shortly.

Noticing Yasmine had finished her wine, Cannon reached for the bottle on the table to pour her another glass.

"Hey, that's enough for now." She held her hand over the glass. "You know what wine does to me." She smiled and sipped her water instead.

He leaned across the candle lit table and answered in a low, seductive tone, "I know exactly what wine does to you."

She bit her bottom lip and cleared her throat. "I think I'll stick to the water."

"Doesn't really matter. We never needed wine to have a good time. So, I hear you're Dr. Dubose now and a professor. How did you go from teaching first grade to college students?"

"It just sort of happened. After I left Nashville, I got my master's at NYU and then my Doctorate in Education. I applied for the adjunct professor position just on a whim. I wanted a change from teaching elementary students, but I didn't want to leave the classroom. So now I teach Language Arts and Literature for Elementary School Teachers."

"Well, I'm not surprised. You've always been determined and goal-oriented. What made you move to Atlanta?"

"I missed the south. It was way too cold in New York, plus I wanted to be closer to my mother. Atlanta is only a six to seven hour drive to Memphis."

"And you've written some books."

"Yes, test prep workbooks geared toward standardized testing, and I also do education consulting for some of the school systems in Metro Atlanta."

"Wow. You seem very busy. Looks like you've turned into a workaholic like me. When do you stop and smell the roses?"

She laughed, and it was great to hear the genuine sound from her. He missed their fun times together. She had always been the spontaneous one in their relationship, making sure no matter how busy he was, he would make time to relax and enjoy life.

"I go out when I can. However, my career does keep me rather busy at times. Being away from Atlanta these past few months has been somewhat of a vacation even though I do part-time consulting for Memphis City Schools. I have a mortgage and bills to pay back home."

He took a sip of his water and leaned back in his chair to stare at her. She was absolutely beautiful, inside and out. He needed to pinch himself to make sure she was truly in front of him. He missed being in her presence.

"What?" she asked with a forehead wrinkle and questionable eyes.

He smiled. "It's really good to see you again. I can't believe you're sitting in front of me."

She gave him a smile that melted his heart. He couldn't fathom he'd spent so many years without it. *What was I thinking letting her go?*

"You are so damn beautiful. I could just sit here for the rest of the night and stare at you."

"Okay, now you're really embarrassing me, but thank you."

"I'll stop … for now." He winked. "I heard your mother was the principal over at our old high school."

"She was, but retired a year ago to concentrate on her health. Luckily, she's better and having fun traveling with her boyfriend. They're out of town for the weekend now."

"Wait. Your mother has a boyfriend?"

"I know. Weird, right? He's a retired principal as well. Very nice man. They've been together for about three years."

"So, does her daughter have a boyfriend?"

It was a question he dreaded knowing the answer to, but he knew she must've had a boyfriend over the past twelve years. The thought of someone else making love to her was impossible in his mind though. Did she moan sweet pleasure sounds in some other guy's ear while digging her fingernails intensely in his shoulders? Did he know about the area on the back of her neck that sent orgasms through her just by a simple touch? Were her climaxes still earth shattering to the point where the only word she could utter was his name? No, wait. Couldn't be, because whomever she'd been with couldn't possibly make her entire body quiver as he had. Didn't love her as he had.

"No, not at the present moment."

"All those successful men in Atlanta and one hasn't wifed you up yet? What are they, blind?"

"I date, and I've had boyfriends over the years but … I don't know," she shrugged, "just haven't found the one."

The band began to play, and Yasmine turned her attention to the stage. Moments later their food arrived, and he was quite surprised when she poured another glass of wine and even asked if he wanted more since his glass was empty. He declined because he'd had a beer earlier while watching a game at the bar.

"So, why haven't you gotten married yet, Dr. Nosey?" she asked.

He grinned. "Like you, I hadn't found the one."

Nodding, she took a sip of her wine. "Zaria seems like a nice lady."

"Zaria the Diva? No. I have my eyes on someone else."

She looked taken aback. "Oh … well do you think you should be out with me tonight?"

"As a matter of fact, yes, considering it's you."

She sighed. "Cannon, we agreed not to go down this road."

"So you can actually look me in my face and tell me you don't feel anything for me?"

With her eyes downcast, she twirled a shrimp around in the grits and then pulled it up with cheese hanging from the fork before placing it back in the bowl.

"No," she said, shaking her head. "I can't tell you that. I'll always care for you. You were a big part of my life for over two years."

It wasn't exactly what he wanted to hear, but at least it was a start in the right direction. He nodded and took a bite of his chicken while she finally ate the shrimp that she'd swished around in the grits.

They ate in silence for the next thirty minutes while listening to the band and finishing their dinner. Justin came over to check on them, bringing out his peach cobbler and homemade vanilla ice cream. After they ate dessert, Yasmine said she needed to head home.

"Thank you for having dinner with me." Cannon leaned on his car facing Yasmine.

"You're welcome." She turned to open her door but hesitated. "I had a really nice time. I'm glad I decided to stay."

"Maybe we can go on another date while you're in town."

She laughed and shook her head. "You just don't quit, do you?"

A slight wind blew and whiffed her perfume mixed with her scent into his nose, bringing his arousal from earlier back to full attention. He stepped toward her.

"Not when I want something." His tone was serious. Direct.

A sexy grin crossed her lips, and she closed the gap between them. "And what is it that you want?"

"You."

And then she smiled that same damn beautiful smile that made him fall in love with her, and he knew he couldn't hold back any longer. He grabbed her hard to him as a gasp flew from her parted lips.

"I've missed the hell out of you, Angel face," he said as he lowered his lips to her trembling ones.

"Show me." Her words were a whisper on his lips.

He kissed her slowly at first, savoring her pouty mouth as she exhaled and moaned. Yasmine meshed her body as hard as possible against his. She pressed into his chest, and he undid the buttons and belt on her trench coat to get a better feel of her against him. He ran a hand down to her breasts, kneading the right one through the satin of her blouse as breathless moans escaped her throat. He plunged his tongue deeper into her mouth, and she willingly accepted it, dancing it around his as she ran her hands along his face and hair. He backed her against his car while lifting one of her legs around his waist as she steadied herself on the other one.

"I missed you," he said in a raspy tone against her mouth. He cupped her face gently and nibbled on her bottom lip. "Missed you like no other." He pushed his hard erection, which was straining against his pants, toward her pelvis so she would know exactly what she was doing to him. She raised her leg even higher on him so his manhood was in between her thighs.

"I missed you too, Cannon," she said, pulling his mouth into hers once more.

He pressed his erection hard against her again and held her still as he cupped her buttocks pulling her toward him. "You feel that?"

"Oh yes!"

"Miss making love to you," he said in between kisses. "Miss being engulfed in you. You hear me, baby?" He ran his tongue down the side of her neck.

"Yes ... Cannon. I've missed you so much."

Her sweet scent and heated kisses were doing him in. He wanted to unzip his pants and slide into her right there against the side of his car, but he'd already seen one SUV pull into the parking lot and some other people leaving when he and Yasmine had first walked outside. Besides, it had been twelve years and their first time after so long wouldn't be there. He wanted her in his bed.

Out of breath, she pulled away from him when they heard voices coming toward the parking lot. Yanking her coat shut, she leaned back against her car.

"I guess we forgot this is a busy parking area," he said as he stepped to pull her against him once more.

"I gotta go." Grabbing her keys from her purse, she hurriedly pressed the remote.

"Wait. What?" He was in shock.

"We can't do this, Cannon." She got into her car. "I can't do this." She shut the door and started her car. He tried to open it, but it was locked. She rolled down the window.

"Yasmine, tell me what's wrong."

She turned her head to him, her eyes glaring with tears. "You hurt me, and I refuse to let you walk back into my life as if you didn't." She backed out of the parking lot as he stared after the car.

What the hell just happened?

CHAPTER SIX

Cannon sat in the VIP section nursing a rum and Coke—mostly rum—and listening to the band play their jazz rendition of Alicia Key's "If I Ain't Got You."

Must they play that? He took another swallow of his drink and slammed it on the table.

After Yasmine sped off with his heart again, he decided to go back into the restaurant considering he had the table for another hour. He wasn't ready to go home yet to another night of needing to be with Yasmine. Ever since Doug had asked him to be the best man, all he could think about was her. Over the years he'd thought of her, but was always able to shut it off with finding something to keep him busy. Now that she was actually in the same city as him, the urge to be near her was wreaking havoc on his brain.

Her sweet scent had filled his aura, and he could still taste the warmth of her on his lips. His hands longed to roam over her body, which had responded to his touch with the same urgency that had built up in him for so many years. It was going to be damn near impossible to stay away from her. His addiction to Yasmine overwhelmed him, and now that he'd had a sample of her, he was feigning for more.

"What's up, man?" he heard a male voice say in front of him, pulling him out of his daydream of Yasmine.

Cannon looked up to see his baby sister, Bria, and her husband, Rasheed Vincent. Bria, who was almost five months pregnant but barely showing, leaned over and kissed him on the forehead. He shook hands with Rasheed who then sat in the opposite chair and pulled his wife onto his lap.

"What brings you two out tonight?" Cannon asked, surprised to see them. "I thought you'd be at home rubbing cocoa butter on your wife's miniature basketball."

"Bria had a craving for crab cakes and some other stuff."

"Memphis mud pie, collard greens, and lobster mac 'n' cheese," she answered, looking through the menu. "Oh and some coconut shrimp."

"Right. All of that." Rasheed laughed. "Save some for the other customers, baby."

"What brings you here by yourself, big brother?" Bria asked. "No date tonight?"

"Let's see, where do I begin?" Cannon downed the rest of his drink and then grabbed the menu to order an appetizer. He wasn't a heavy drinker for he hated not being alert at all times.

"Wait, is this going to be a long story? Because I'll probably need to go to the ladies' room soon."

"Bree, you went before we left the house," Rasheed said, rubbing his wife's belly.

She cut her eyes at him and said in a teasing manner, "Is your uterus pressing on your bladder?"

"No, not exactly," her husband said before turning to Cannon. "Man, hurry up and tell the damn story. What girl got you in here all melancholy and what not?"

He quickly told them about eating dinner with Yasmine, kissing her and her speeding away like he was the black plague.

Bria stood and kissed Rasheed's forehead. "Gotta go to the ladies' room. Baby, you know what to order."

"Everything but the kitchen sink?" Rasheed asked with a wink.

"Ha! Very funny."

Cannon smiled at the back and forth playful banter between Bria and Rasheed. Cannon was elated when she announced they were getting married. Before her husband, she was in a relationship with a man that lied and cheated on her during most of their relationship. The last straw was right before they were supposed to get married, the guy finally admitted that not only had he cheated but his side chick was pregnant. Bria was devastated, and it took willpower for Cannon and Sean to not throw the guy in the Mississippi River.

At first, Cannon wasn't too sure he like Rasheed either. He was a famous, retired basketball player with the reputation of being a player extraordinaire on and off the court. Everyone in Memphis knew he changed his women like underwear. However, Rasheed wanted a woman who loved him for him and not his millions, which was why he kept a merry-go-round of women. Bria didn't care about his money, and after working out her trust issues and falling for his game of seduction, she realized that Rasheed was the only man for her.

"Bria showed me a picture a while back of you and Yasmine," Rasheed said after the waitress left with his long order. "You two looked really happy together. Especially you. I've seen you with other women, but that smile you wore while gazing at Yasmine, I've never witnessed before."

"Yasmine was very special to me. Still is, but she doesn't want to have anything to do with me."

"Naw, man, I disagree. If she truly didn't want anything to do with you, she'd make sure to never see you doing the planning of this wedding."

"We don't have a choice."

"Trust me. Women will find ways to avoid you. Besides, she kissed you and then ran off, which means she definitely still has feelings for you."

"I just thought by now she would've forgiven me."

"Bree briefly told me what happened years ago. She may have forgiven you, but women don't forget anything. Trust me. Every blue moon Bria likes to remind me about the time when we were in the car and a stripper called about her and some of her girls dancing for me. I wasn't even interested, but Bria will never let that go. She says it in a teasing manner, but I know she isn't teasing."

"Teasing about what?"

The men were so engrossed in their conversation, that they didn't see Bria return. She sat back on her husband's lap with a raised eyebrow.

"Nothing, babe. Just talking about Cannon's dilemma," Rasheed said with a wicked grin.

"Humph. Sure you are," Bria said, thumping Rasheed playfully on the cheek. "Cannon, I think you may want to give her some space. She obviously still cares about you, but women don't like to unexpectedly run into their ex boyfriend's without a plan. Plus, you're planning a wedding together, which is what you were doing when you broke up. I'm sure that has brought back a lot of unwanted memories that she has buried."

Cannon nodded and sipped on his water. "Okay, so give her some space. I can do that." *Right?* He wasn't sure if he believed himself or not considering he just wanted to jump into his car and drive straight to her house to finish what they'd started in the parking lot.

"I would take it slow. Don't rush anything if you really want her back."

"I hear you, sis."

Cannon sat back and listened to the music for a while before leaving the love birds. He decided to play it cool and give Yasmine some space … but only a little.

Yasmine sat on the deck overlooking the Mississippi River, sipping hot chocolate and trying to figure out how she got herself into this mess. She was back in the place she was a few years ago where the need of wanting Cannon so badly consumed her thoughts and invaded her sleep. She'd daydreamed about him, dreamed about him, and even went so far as to search for him on the Internet. She found journals he'd written and documentaries about the medical clinics he had opened with Doctors Unlimited, the non-profit organization he founded with some other doctors after his yearlong mission trip to Brazil.

She hadn't realized just how much he'd contributed to the medical field. She knew it was important to him because of his family background, but seeing him on the documentaries helping children with infectious diseases, made her see that she'd made the best decision in letting him go.

A few days before he was scheduled to leave, she'd received a voicemail from Cannon telling her that he loved her and he wouldn't go to Brazil for a year if she really didn't want him to. She played the message almost a hundred times over the course of two days before deleting it without returning his phone call. She loved him dearly, but she wasn't going to be selfish and stand in his way of his dreams.

Sometimes, over the years, she'd regretted her decision for she hated being without him. She missed the little things, like sitting in his lap and resting her head on his chest just to hear her favorite song—his heartbeat. Or gliding her finger along the scar on the left side of his chest. He'd gotten it as a child from a bike accident and if it had just been a few inches deeper, it could have pierced his heart. That always haunted her for she couldn't imagine life without him even if he was only in it for a few years. She swallowed remembering the way she used to be obsessed over it. He always found it funny, but never complained when she would kiss, lick, or run her finger around the scar.

Nevertheless, when she saw the documentaries a few years ago, she knew she had made the right decision in not calling him back, for if she had heard his voice in her ear or seen him in person, she would've begged him not to go. Even though she no longer regretted letting him go—well sometimes—it hurt like hell to be without him.

Now here he was back in her life, and she didn't know what to do with her roller coaster of emotions. Tonight he reminded her just how much she loved and missed him, but she was scared. She had to remember, despite her feelings for him, he still hurt her by pushing aside their wedding plans just as he had done everything else while they were together.

The vibrating of her cell phone startled her out of her thoughts. She was relieved to see that it was Sherika and not Cannon.

"Hey, girl!"

"Hey, Yaz. I got the pictures of the floral arrangements and emailed Zaria back. I love them so much!"

"I'm glad it all worked out." The warmth of the hot chocolate was wearing off, so Yasmine went back inside and sat in front of the lit fireplace.

"I'll say! You and Cannon just saved me $700. Please, tell him thank you the next time you see or talk to him."

"Uh … sure. Sure will."

"Oh oh. What happened?"

Yasmine laughed nervously. "Nothing. So what else do you need me to do?" Yasmine grabbed her notepad from the coffee table that had her things to do list.

"Girl, even though I'm completely stressing over this wedding, I still care about what is going on with you and Cannon. I know planning this wedding with him has to be hard."

"We agreed to be cordial and everything was going okay, but then I let my guard down, and he kissed me and it felt so good to be in his arms again with his lips on mine. I didn't know just how much I missed being with him, smelling him, touching him." Tears welled up in her eyes again, but she brushed them away. She hadn't cried over him in years, and she didn't feel like starting now.

"Oh my goodness! This is wonderful. Wait? Is he there now? Am I disturbing something?"

"No. I … um … sort of pushed him off of me, got in my car, and left him standing in the parking lot with a puzzled look on his face."

"Girl, what am I going to do with you? You know Cannon still loves you. Doug said he never got over you, but like you, he went on with his life. I think if there is still something there to pursue, then do it. Doug and I were friends for years after we dated for a few months, but when he moved to New York last year, we just knew we were meant to be. I can't imagine being without him."

"Your story is different. Doug never hurt you, and he wants you to go with him to Madrid. Cannon never asked me to go to Brazil with him. He just brushed off our wedding and said we could get married anytime after he returned."

"Would you have gone if he'd asked?"

"Sherika, I don't know. What would I have done over there?"

"Teach and be with your man. But that's coulda woulda shoulda. The question is what are you going to do now that he's back in your life and apparently still has feelings for you?"

"I don't know. Let's change the subject."

"Okay. You have your pen and paper ready?"

Yasmine laughed and positioned her pen to write. "I'm ready, bridezilla."

"So, after looking at the pictures Zaria sent, I've decided to go with all white flowers tied in fuchsia ribbons for me, you, and the bridesmaids. Also, I've decided that I want you and the bridesmaids to wear white dresses as well."

"So everyone is wearing white?" Yasmine hated asking the question as if Sherika was out of her mind, but it was her wedding.

"Not everyone. The groom and his party will still wear black tuxedos, but instead of the fuchsia vest and rosebud, they will be white."

"Cool. I believe the groomsmen will be happy about not having to wear pink vests."

"Yeah, I know. That's what Doug said. I'm going to email you some dresses to look at."

"Okay. I'm meeting your cousins next week at the bridal shop you picked to get measured and try on dresses."

"Mmmm ... I believe Cannon and Doug's brothers are going to the tuxedo shop next door. The wedding coordinator said the shops are owned by the same person and that the wedding party is receiving fifteen percent off."

"Lovely, I get to possibly see Cannon again," Yasmine said sarcastically.

"Maybe not."

"Trust me. He'll be there looking at me through the window."

"Whatever, Yaz. You know you love it."

"I know I love my peace of mind that I haven't had lately. Instead, it's crowded with thoughts of Cannon."

"That's nothing new. Anyway, Doug and I will be there in a few weeks to meet with the coordinator, do the reception tasting and meet with the pastor in person. We've been Skyping our counseling sessions."

"So glad you're coming. Think we'll have time to go to the spa? My treat."

"Yes, I could use a massage and apparently you can as well. Of course you'd rather have your massage from Cannon."

"I'm ignoring you. Anything else, Madame Bride?"

"Nope, that's it for now. Going to go cuddle with Doug. Maybe if you made a phone call, you could be cuddling, too."

After she hung up the phone with Sherika, Yasmine grabbed a glass of wine and soaked in a bubble bath, hoping that would ease her mind and body from her long day. Unfortunately, every time she closed her eyes, all she saw was Cannon kissing her and roaming his hands aggressively over her body how she needed him to.

CHAPTER SEVEN

The phone ringing jolted Yasmine from under the covers even though she wasn't getting any sleep. She'd tossed and turned all night over that stupid kiss in the parking lot. Her heart was angry for leaving him because she wanted him just as much as he wanted her, but her head kept telling her to be sensible. Now she wished she'd listened to her heart.

She answered her cell phone not recognizing the number on the screen. She kind of hoped it was Cannon.

"Hello?"

"Hi, Yasmine?" an unfamiliar female's voice asked.

"Yes?"

"This is Lacy, your mother's mentee."

"Oh, hello, Lacy." Yasmine was sort of disappointed it wasn't Cannon. She'd met Lacy a few times while she'd been back in Memphis. Lacy was a twenty-two year old single mother with a five year old daughter. Yasmine's mother had taken Lacy under her wing through a mentoring program sponsored by her sorority.

She got out of the bed and headed downstairs to make a pot of coffee since there was no point in staying in the bed any longer. "How are you?"

"Not good. I called your mother forgetting she was out of town, and she suggested I call you and gave me your cell number."

"No problem. What's wrong?"

"It's my daughter. She has a high fever and can't keep any food down."

"Perhaps you should take her to the emergency room. What hospital are you near? I can meet you there."

"I don't have any insurance, and I'm low on cash at the moment. But there's a clinic that allows walk-ins and doesn't charge too much. I can take the bus there."

"No, I'll come get you." She paused, thinking about a better solution. "You know what? Let me call you right back, but still get ready."

After she hung up with Lacy, Yasmine took a deep breath and called the only pediatrician she knew.

"Hello?" he answered.

"Hey, it's me," she said in a quiet tone. She almost felt bad about calling him, considering she'd left him in the cold last night, but she knew the kind of man he was and would put aside their differences to help someone in need.

"Well … hey there, *me*. I wasn't expecting to hear from you."

"Are you busy?"

"No. Just sitting here wondering why you sped off last night."

"I didn't call to discuss that, but I promise we will soon. Right now, I have a medical emergency."

"What's wrong, Angel face?"

She smiled at the urgency and sincerity in his voice as well as the nickname he used to call her. "No, not me. My mother's mentee's daughter has a really high fever and can't keep any food down. She doesn't have insurance, and she mentioned a clinic but that could take hours."

"Enough said. Tell her to meet me at Arrington Family Specialists. I'll leave here in ten minutes and should be there in about twenty to thirty minutes."

"She doesn't have a car so I'm picking them up. It may be an hour before we get there."

"No problem. Where do they live?"

"I remember my mom saying the Channing Hill area. I'll find out when I call back."

"No, you're not going over there by yourself. I'm coming to get you. I keep an emergency bag in my car so I'll just exam her there."

"Cannon, I'll be fine." She shrugged as she walked back upstairs to get dressed. She didn't see the big deal. She used to visit friends in that area all the time in high school and never had any problems.

"Yasmine, you haven't lived here in years. The Channing area has gotten worse."

"But—"

"It's not up for debate," he said in a concise tone. "I'll be at your house in twenty minutes."

She smiled to herself as she remembered him always saying "it's not up for debate" to imply the conversation had ended, and it was going to be his way or no way. His take charge attitude had always made her feel protected so she trusted that he knew what he was doing in this situation.

While she waited for Cannon, she called her mother so she wouldn't be worried about Lacy and her daughter.

"So, you called Cannon?" Emma Dubose asked inquisitively. She'd been very saddened by their break up because Cannon had been like a son to her when he was in high school. When Yasmine had told her she was dating him and then engaged, Mrs. Dubose was ecstatic to learn that he would officially be part of the family.

"Yes, Mother. He's on his way to pick me up." Yasmine flipped through the clothes in her closet for something quick to throw on. She decided on jeans and a sweater with tennis shoes. She took off her satin cap, ran her hands through her pixie cut, and then jetted downstairs to wait for Cannon. She had a feeling he'd be on time.

"Oh really? I see he's still the chivalrous rescuer."

"Mother, this isn't about us. It's about helping Lacy."

"Well, I'm glad Cannon was available."

"Me too."

"So are you two getting along in planning the wedding?"

"Just can't wait for it to be over with."

"Well … you seem a little happier that he's back in your life."

"Mom …" She really didn't want to have this conversation with her mother. She knew her mom would be overjoyed if they got back together, considering she'd hinted at it since she found out they would help plan Sherika's wedding.

"I just want you happy and if anything were to ever happen to me, I don't want you to be alone."

Yasmine's heart broke. "Mom, please don't speak like that." She sat down on the front step and placed her head on her knees. "You're not leaving me anytime soon. Your cancer is in remission."

"I know, darling, but sometimes I wish you had a husband and children. When I was sick, all I kept thinking was who will take care of my baby if I die."

"But you didn't die, and I know how to take care of myself. I don't need a man for that. I've been taking care of me for a very long time."

"I know. I just worry about you sometimes being alone in Atlanta with no family. I know you date, but when was the last time you were in a serious relationship?"

"A few years ago. You remember Daniel, Mom."

"I was hoping you two would get married, but as soon as he mentioned children, you dropped him."

"Mom, I dropped him because of his misogynistic and male chauvinist thinking. He wanted me to quit work and be a stay at home mom until the children graduated high school, all five of them by the way. I didn't earn four degrees to stay at home."

"Since Cannon, you've broken up with guys before they got too close to your heart to break it or found some reason why they weren't good enough. I just want you to be happy."

"Mother, I promise you, I'm happy. I have a wonderful career, family, friends and a beautiful home in Atlanta. Most importantly, I have you. A healthy, cancer-free mother who isn't leaving me anytime soon."

"You're darn right, I'm not. However, you seem happier since Cannon has been back in your life. And who knows. Maybe it is fate."

That was the second time in two days she'd heard "maybe it is fate." She didn't see it like that. She saw it as a cruel joke that she just needed to get through so she could move back to Atlanta and back to her life without him.

She looked up to see a black car slow down and pull into the driveway.

"Mom, I have to go. He's here." She stood and grabbed her purse off of the step. Cannon got out of the car and walked to the passenger's side to open the door.

"Send Lacy my love. I'll call later to check on her."

"I will, Mother. Have fun with your man." She slid onto the heated black leather seat, which was perfect after sitting on the cold porch.

"Trust me, I am," Emma said in sassy tone. "You do the same."

"I'm ignoring that last statement. In fact, I'm ignoring both." She wanted her mother happy, but she didn't want to imagine her mother having "fun" with her man.

"You can't ignore love, my dear."

They said their good-byes, and Yasmine tossed her cell phone into her purse, setting it on the floor of the car.

"Hey," Cannon said as he closed his door and put on his seat belt.

"Thank you so much for doing this for me on your day off. Mother and I sincerely appreciate it."

"You're welcome, and a doctor never has a day off."

Cannon and Yasmine rode in silence on the way to Lacy's apartment. She was happy to know that Yasmine was bringing a pediatrician.

She didn't know what to say especially after her conversation with her mother. She knew her mother worried about her being happy, but overall life had been good. Just because she wasn't with the one man she'd ever truly loved didn't mean she wasn't happy. It just meant she didn't have everything she wanted, but she had everything she needed. *Right?*

Yasmine stared at Cannon. He was definitely in doctor mode as he pondered over what could be wrong with Lacy's daughter just by what Yasmine had told him. She remembered that mode when he was in medical school studying at her kitchen table into the wee hours of the morning.

"She doesn't have insurance," Yasmine said, remembering what Lacy had told her. "She works part-time because she's in college, so just send me the bill."

He looked at her out of the corner of his eye and chuckled. "Do you know me?"

"I beg your pardon?"

"Yasmine, what have I been doing practically all of my life? You think I'm a doctor because of the money?"

She shook her head. "No. You're a doctor because you want to help people."

"Exactly. My parents instilled in me and my siblings when we were growing up to always give back, to be active and positive role models in the community. My dad grew up in poverty. He watched his mother die when he was only sixteen because she couldn't afford proper medical care. Trust me, my dad would ring my neck if I even thought about taking money from someone who needs medical attention but can't afford it."

Once they arrived at the apartment complex, she caught him glancing at her neck and her hands.

"What?" she asked, wondering why he kept looking over her body.

"Take off your Movado and your necklace." He leaned over and opened the glove compartment. "Lock them in here. You can leave your earrings on." He reached out and touched her sterling silver hoops. His finger brushed her cheek and a sensual connection locked their eyes together before he dropped his hand. "What kind of purse is that?" He pointed to the bag at her feet.

"A Coach."

"Place it in the back under my white coats that need to go to the cleaners."

"Why am I doing all this?" she asked, putting her jewelry in the compartment. She shut it, and he pushed a button on the dash to lock it.

"You don't want to draw too much attention to yourself."

"So what are you going to do, push a button to turn your top of the line BMW invisible?"

He laughed. "No, not quite. It will be fine. I promise."

She didn't answer, but instead placed her purse under his white coats and then got out of the car when he did. He popped the trunk, grabbing a bag and a small ice cooler. He shut it, looked around for a second, and nodded as a bodyguard-looking guy strolled over. He had a "don't-mess-with-me" look and was at least six foot six.

"What's up, doc?" The men shook hands. "How you living?"

"Can't complain. Glad you were around when I called. Thank you."

"No problem. If I wasn't here, I would've made sure one of my boys would be. Don't worry. We got you."

"I appreciate it."

"Your pops and Dr. Raven were down to the community center with some other doctors last week doing free health screenings and physicals. My levels still look good."

Cannon nodded. "He mentioned that to me, but I wasn't able to get down here. Had an emergency at the hospital."

"Well, I'll be right here."

"Thank you. We'll be back."

As they walked toward Lacy's apartment building, Yasmine stopped them halfway. "Is he watching your car?" she asked, as she glanced back to see the guy sitting on a bench near the parking lot. They continued walking and Cannon didn't answer.

"So apparently they know you and your dad over here?" she acknowledged as she saw some other people wave and nod their heads toward him.

"Yes. This is where my dad lived in his teen years. He promised to come back and help in any way, so we all do. The guy that's watching my car, I saved his daughter's life two years ago. However, my car was broken into while I was doing so and my rims were stolen as well. Watching my car is his way of paying me."

An hour later they were back in the car and headed to Yasmine's house. She was glad she called him after all. Lacy's daughter had a stomach virus that was going around at her school. Cannon gave her some Pedialyte and children's Tylenol with instructions and his work cell phone number should she need anything else.

"Thank you. I'm so glad you were available on a Sunday afternoon," Yasmine said as they sat in her driveway.

"No problem. When's your mother coming back in town?"

"Tuesday. They're in Fort Lauderdale."

"Are you hungry? I'm starved. You called right when I was going to make lunch and now it is dinner time." He glanced at the clock on the dashboard.

"I was going to make salmon today. There's plenty for the two of us along with a salad."

"No wonder you're pretty much the same size as when I met you. You eat like a bird."

"No, I eat what I want and work out, but I have a dress fitting next week. Carbs go straight to my hips."

"How about I take you out to eat?"

"I don't mind making dinner. It will be my way of saying thank you for helping Lacy. I can add baked potatoes to the meal, and I believe there's still some Oreo cheesecake left."

"Now you're talking."

Cannon sat on a barstool at the kitchen island while Yasmine cut up cucumbers for their salads. They made small talk while she cooked, staying on topics related to politics and education. However, tonight they were going to have it out whether she wanted to or not, he decided.

"The salmon should be done in about fifteen minutes," she said, taking off her apron and setting it on the island. She gave him his bowl of salad and retrieved a bottle of wine from the refrigerator.

"White zinfandel?" she asked, showing him the bottle.

"Perfect. I'll open it for you."

She handed him the wine and the corkscrew while she took two wine glasses from the cabinet.

"I can't believe this is the same house."

"Yep, my mother had everything remodeled," she said, looking around the updated kitchen with cherry wood cabinets, black granite counter tops, and stainless steel appliances. "She should've just bought a new home, but she has memories of my dad here and didn't want to leave. Plus, she loves living by the river."

"How does it feel to be back home with your mother?" He poured the wine as she sat on the bar stool across the island from him.

"Well at first, I didn't think about it because I was here for her chemo treatments. Before I decided to take the sabbatical from work, I would drive up every week and stay a few days, but I hated leaving her afterwards. I know she has her boyfriend, and he's been wonderful, but she's my mother. She's all I have. So I decided to move back temporarily. She's been in remission since November, but I didn't want to leave until I felt as if she had truly recovered. She's stronger now, gaining some weight back, and her hair is starting to grow again. I cut mine really short when hers began to fall out."

"I was wondering why you cut your hair. I know you've always preferred it long."

"It'll grow back. Anyway, it does feel weird sleeping in my old room. Besides college breaks, I haven't really lived here since I was eighteen."

"I remember when we used to come visit our families when we lived in Nashville. We slept in your twin canopy bed because you just had to sleep in your own room and not the guestroom." Cannon laughed as he remembered the pink walls, pink and green comforter set with the huge pink flowers, pink fluffy pillows and the pink canopy over the bed. "All that damn pink. I felt like I was in a bottle of Pepto Bismol."

"It was hilarious, both of us trying to fit in that

bed." She laughed, taking a sip of her wine. "But there's a queen bed in there now with no canopy, and the walls are beige."

"Didn't we break the bed one time?"

"Ha! Yes. One of the bed rails came unattached from the headboard."

"Yeah, I remember. I fixed it and then pulled you down on the floor to finish making love to you."

She lowered her eyes. "Cannon, let's not do this right now."

He slid off of the barstool and pulled her into his arms, deciding to forgo Bria's suggestion of giving Yasmine space. He needed her and besides, if she wanted space, she wouldn't have invited him to stay for dinner.

"You mean you don't remember? I do. We didn't want to wake your mother, so I started off with slow strokes so you and the bed wouldn't make a sound. More so you. Then you kept telling me how damn good I was making you feel, and I got a little faster and the rail came loose, but luckily your mother didn't hear. We waited a few minutes to make sure, and then I put the comforter and the pillows on the floor. I was able to give you long, deep thrusts from behind as you buried your head in the pillow to muffle out just how good it was."

She tried to step out of his embrace, but he held her firm next to him. He could hear her heart beating faster and louder. "Tell me you don't remember that night."

"I remember," she said with a smirk. "You had to use the pillow as well in the end."

"We had some great times, Yasmine."

She exhaled. "Yes, we did ... but—"

"But what? I know you still feel something for me."

"I—"

"It's in your voice. It's in your eyes. It's in your heart."

"Cannon—"

"I miss you saying my name." He kissed her softly on the side of her neck, releasing a sensual moan. "Miss you moaning in my ear." He lifted the bottom of her sweater up, running his hands up her back and then down to her butt, pulling her into him. "Miss your skin next to mine." He continued trailing kisses down her neck. "Miss your scent."

He claimed her lips in an erotic kiss, sinking his tongue deep inside of her mouth, sending sizzling currents through his body that he was pretty sure she felt as she trembled in his arms.

"Why did you leave me last night?" He kissed her quivering lips hard, needing to claim her again. He wanted to kiss away the memory of the men that came after him.

"I was scared." Her words were a breathless whisper.

"I wanted you. Needed you so bad. I was up half the night trying to force myself to not hop in my car and come over here. Tell me what I have to do to make you mine again."

Pushing away from him, she walked to the other side of the island.

She shook her head and answered him in a soft tone, "I don't know. You hurt me." Her voice escalated to an irritated pitch. "You left me."

"I didn't intentionally leave you. I was coming back, and may I remind you, you called off our engagement not me. I never said I didn't want to marry you."

"No," she lashed out. "You said we could get married anytime and then told me you weren't ready to get married." She sighed and all the pain he'd caused was plain as day on her face. "How do you think that made me feel?"

"I'm so sorry for hurting you. I had a lot on my plate, and I wasn't thinking about—"

"Me." Her voice was barely above a whisper. "You weren't thinking about me."

"You didn't deserve to be treated that way."

"No I didn't, considering I put you first in my life."

"And you did. I took for granted that you'd always be by my side no matter what."

She looked away from him for a second before settling her eyes on his face with a heartbreaking stare. "Maybe we simply weren't meant to be." Her voice cracked and she looked away, blinking back tears that he didn't want to fall. He hated seeing her cry knowing he was the cause of her pain.

"Is that what you think?" he questioned, as he stepped around the island to stand directly in front of her. "That we weren't meant to be?"

"No, but if you keep telling yourself something over and over you start to believe it as the truth. I loved you very much, Cannon, and I wanted nothing more than to spend the rest of my life with you, but you had other plans that didn't include me. It hurt like hell when you walked out that door."

"Didn't you get my last voicemail? I waited and waited for you to call back. Even at the airport I looked around thinking you'd come."

"I thought about it, but I couldn't be selfish. So I didn't run after you. I wasn't going to beg you not to go. You had this wonderful opportunity to go to Brazil and help open the clinic in that impoverished village that needed medical care. You worked so hard to make it happen."

"Yasmine, I was coming back. I wasn't going to be in Brazil forever. I had my residency to come back to and you."

"I know, but you would've just found something else to get involved with. I've kept up with you over years. I've read all of your articles and seen the documentaries that were done on the other clinics you've helped set up in other countries. You've contributed a lot to the medical field by starting Doctors Unlimited."

"Well, you did tell me to go save the world."

She laughed, but suddenly tears started to run down her face. "I did, but in the end, I just didn't see where I would fit in with your life."

He pulled her to him and kissed her forehead. "But you did. You were the one thing in my life that was stable. You kept me focused and motivated. After we broke up, I was a wreck, woman."

"That may be true, but you blatantly told me you weren't ready to get married, and we could get married *anytime* as if marrying me was the last thing on your list to do."

"I never meant to hurt you, Yasmine."

"I know," she said softly and laid her head on his chest.

"I messed up." He shook his head and raised her chin so she could see he meant every word. "No, I didn't mess up. I fucked up. I lost the only woman I've ever loved, and I don't want to lose you again."

"Cannon, it's not that easy." She tried to pull away from his embrace, but he held her firm in his arms, refusing to let her get away from him again.

"Tell me you don't love me anymore, and I'll leave you alone. However, I still love you very much, Angel face, and will until the day I die."

Tears cascaded down her face and a heavenly smile crossed her lips. "I still love you very much, too. I've hated being apart from you, but after seeing all the wonderful things you've done with Doctors Unlimited. I'd do it again. I don't regret it."

"I promise to never give you a reason again, Angel face."

"Oh how I've missed you calling me that."

She jumped up into his arms, latching her lips onto his in the process and releasing a passionate avalanche of kisses on him. He placed her on the island as she wrapped her legs around his middle. He could feel her quiver in his arms as he penetrated her mouth deeply with his tongue, sending waves of sensual fire through his loins. He kissed her in a commanding manner as he molded his mouth into hers. He was going to do his damndest this time to kiss her senseless. No running away from him like last night. She was his, and with every stroke of his tongue, he was going to make sure she realized that. She whispered his name, and he closed his mouth over hers as she surrendered a moan.

"You're all mine again, you hear me?" he said, nibbling on her bottom lip.

"Yes and no." She gave him a lazy smile even though he didn't find it quite funny. *Didn't we just express that we're still in love with each other?*

"Are you trying to give me a heart attack?" He placed his hands over his heart and stumbled back a little, laughing at the same time. "Elizabeth, I'm coming to join you honey."

She laughed for a few moments at his Fred Sanford impersonation before speaking in a serious yet sincere tone. "No, just listen. I don't want to rush into anything with you because even though we still love each other, we may be in love with the younger versions of us when we first started dating."

Resting his palms on either side of her on top of the island, he pressed his forehead against hers. "Please explain."

"We've both changed and matured over the past twelve years. Instead of rushing, perhaps we should take it one day at a time and get to know each other again."

He nodded reluctantly. "I suppose I understand where you're coming from. I mean, you may have picked up some annoying bad habit that I can't stand," he said with a wink.

She playfully punched him on the arm. "Very funny, but the same can go for you as well. Oh, and I have a three month rule now," she said. The timer, which had been beeping off and on for the past ten minutes, beeped again. Sliding off of the island, she walked toward the oven, and pulled out the salmon that was definitely done. She placed the pan next to the baked potatoes on the counter.

"Three month rule for what? Going to get your teeth cleaned? Your oil changed? Tires rotated?"

She smirked and placed a piece of salmon on his plate. "No, silly. Sex. I've been celibate for a while now, but when I do date seriously, I just don't jump into bed with every Tom, Dick, and Harry right away."

"Well, I hope not but um … you didn't wait three months with me." He encircled his arms around her waist and placed his chin on her shoulder while she cut the baked potatoes in half. It felt good to hold her that way again.

"I know." Yasmine turned to look back at him with a grin on her face. "You're the reason why I have the rule."

"Ouch. I see your sarcastic sense of humor hasn't changed."

"I'm not teasing."

CHAPTER EIGHT

Over the next few weeks, Cannon spent all of his free time after work with Yasmine either running errands for the wedding, just chilling at home, or going out. He was still somewhat in shock over her three month rule, but he was going to honor it—or at least try. Even though he knew there were some times he sensed she wanted to break it.

Tonight, Yasmine was on her way over to make the wedding favors. He'd printed the labels for the miniature bubble bottles that she was bringing along with the pink ribbon to tie around the top of it. He chuckled to himself as he thought about every time he said pink she would correct him by saying its fuchsia. Pink. Fuchsia. Hot pink. To him it was all just pink.

She arrived on time; that was one thing about her that definitely had not changed. She was always punctual and hated being late to anything. Unfortunately, once home, time restraints were nonexistent to him until his alarm clock sounded in the morning.

Cannon heard the doorbell ring just as he walked back into the kitchen from doing a few laps in his indoor heated pool. He thought he'd have time to change because all he had on were his swim trunks. He glanced on the monitor in the keeping room on the way to the front door. She looked frustrated, holding bags and a box she had readjusted to ring the doorbell again.

"Hey there," he said, opening the door and grabbing the box from her.

She ran her eyes over his semi-naked body. Her gaze settled on his chest and he moved his pecs, which released a pretty smile from her. He saw her glance at the scar on the left side of his chest, and she sucked in her breath before turning to shut the door. He found it cute she was the only woman ever to be fascinated with the scar left from a few stitches.

"About time. I was getting ready to leave."

"I can always give you a key," he said as he led the way to the kitchen table where he had everything set up for them to make the wedding favors.

"Is this an ice breaker game for the evening?" She ran her fingers down his back, which was sure to provoke another lap—or ten—in the pool. "Why are you answering the door half naked trying to be smooth and sexy in your swim trunks?"

"So you think I'm smooth and sexy?" He winked at her and took the bag she had on her wrist.

"I said trying to be." She smiled before kissing his cheek.

"Well, you keep touching me like that and you'll see how smooth I can be in the bedroom. I'm sure you remember."

She shook her head, laughing nervously. "Go get dressed."

"All right. I'll be back in a few minutes, unless you want to join me in the shower." He lowered his head and gave her a slow, sensual kiss.

"As tempting as that is," she ran her finger over his scar and then patted him on his butt, "no." She winked and stepped out of his embrace.

"You know you want all of this," he teased as he headed toward the staircase. "There's some pita bread and hummus in the refrigerator for you and some sliced cantaloupes."

"Thanks. I'll set it on the island so we won't get food on the favors."

Twenty minutes later they had an assembly line going at the kitchen table. He placed the labels on the bubble bottles, and she tied the ribbon around the top before placing them in a huge white basket. Around the handle was an artificial vine of white roses intertwined with ivy leaves topped with a huge fuchsia bow.

"How many?" he asked in a tired tone after the twentieth one.

"You already know we have two hundred and fifty to do. After that, it's on to the bird seed and tulle baggies." She pointed to the bag on the floor.

"We must *really* love our best friends," he said with a chuckle as he passed her another bottle.

"We do. Besides, they would do the same for us if we were getting married." She stopped tying the bow on the bottle and raised her head slowly to meet his eyes.

"Really?" he asked as she lowered her eyes to finish tying the bow. "Is that our next step?"

"Cannon, we've only been back in each other's lives for a few months, and we aren't even a couple. Marriage should be the last thing on our minds."

He sighed. "I know. We're in the getting-to-know-each-other stage again." He rolled his eyes.

"Are you being sarcastic?"

"No, I'm being serious. However, just so you know, eventually I will ask you to marry me, Yasmine. I told you, I'm never letting you go again, so you might as well get used to this."

She pursed her lips together to smother a smile, but ended up releasing a beautiful one instead. "You just won't quit."

"Not this time. So let's change the subject. Tell me about the men you've dated since me."

She went to the island where their snacks were and scooped up some hummus on a pita cracker.

"I know you're joking," she sarcastically said with a wrinkled brow. "You don't really want to know."

"Just curious." He set a few more labeled bottles on her side of the table.

She sighed, popped another cracker in her mouth, and proceeded to wash her hands before returning to the assembly line.

"Well, let's see. Your rebound was a stockbroker I met when I first moved to New York. Nice guy, I suppose. A little on the arrogant side, but not toward me. Smoked cigars. Took me to the Hamptons one summer."

"What happened? He seemed like a good catch." *Okay, she's right. I really don't want to know.*

"I wasn't ready for a commitment. The guy after him was a jazz musician. Played the saxophone. Drove a motorcycle. He was cool, but our schedules were different. He was at work when I needed to be asleep."

"Um ... you never went to see him perform?"

"Sometimes on the weekends, but rarely during the week. I had grad school, and I taught second grade. My career came first which was his gripe. He said I was heartless, lacked warmth, and wasn't supportive of his dreams. Come to think of it, the stockbroker said the same and another guy I dated."

"I find it hard to believe that someone said you lacked warmth and was heartless. You're the most loving person I know."

"You can believe it because I know I was all those things." She sighed. "I didn't want another man to get so close to me that I fell in love only to get hurt again. I put up a wall that none of them could knock down or climb over."

"So you haven't been in love with anyone else besides me?"

"Don't flatter yourself. Kinda hard to fall in love when you left your heart with someone else. You're the only man that has ever broken it, and I didn't want to experience it again."

"Damn, I made you bitter?"

"I wasn't bitter. I dated and had fun, but a woman has to protect herself as well."

"I can respect that considering I have three sisters. I would kill a man over them. That guy who broke Bria's heart better be glad she begged me and Sean not to go over to his house to have a men to punk conversation."

"Really? Too bad I don't have a big brother. Maybe he would've done that for me." She yawned. "How many more?"

"Plenty."

"Cool. I need a break. What do you have at the bar?" she asked, walking over to the butler's pantry between the kitchen and the dining room.

"Just about anything. You know I pretty much only drink rum and Coke, but I believe there's some Crown in the cabinet."

"My favorite." She found it in the bottom cabinet and took a can of Coke out of the mini fridge.

He rewound their conversation in his head a few times before meeting her in the butler's pantry.

"Wait a minute. You would've sent your big brother over to have a conversation with me?" he asked half laughing, but half scared of her answer.

She smirked. "I guess we'll never know." She patted his cheek and went back to the table.

They continued to work in silence for a while, taking short breaks to rest their hands and to make sure they wouldn't mess up.

"The last one," she said tossing it in the basket with the other two-hundred and forty nine bottles of bubbles.

"We did a good job," he said, reaching across the table and giving her a high five. "Maybe we should go into the wedding business. I think we've done more work than the wedding planner."

"I know, right?" She took the basket and set it on the dining room table before grabbing the packs of bird seed along with the box of tulle bags. "So since you were being Dr. Nosey, what about the women *you've* dated since me?" She slid back into her chair, sipped her drink, and then downed it.

A slow grin crossed his face. "I was wondering when you were going to ask me."

Leaning back, she closed her eyes for a second and breathed in deep. "Go ahead."

"Well, let's see. I met a nurse during my residency. We just hung out, you know. Then there was this other girl. She was cool. We dated until I moved back to Memphis."

"What happened?"

"She didn't want a long distance relationship. About a few years ago, I was in a serious relationship. She kept pressuring me into marrying her, showing me rings and talking about how many children we would have. Shelbi thinks my ex was trying to get pregnant because she kept forgetting to take her pill on time or not at all."

"Why didn't you marry her?"

"She wasn't you."

Yasmine breathed out a sigh of relief at his answer. Over the years, she'd always wondered about his dating life. Was he in love? Was he married? And when she found out he wasn't married—why wasn't he married? She secretly wanted to believe that she was the reason. That he still loved her. That he couldn't possibly marry another woman because like her, his heart was somewhere else.

"Come here," she whispered in a sexy voice.

A sly smile crossed his face as he pulled her out of the chair and into his arms.

Cannon's mouth hurriedly, seductively imprisoned hers. His arms squeezed around her, drawing her against his hard frame. She happily welcomed the feel of his exploring tongue on her lips as he delved in even more. Wave after wave of pure bliss charged through her body, awakening the long-buried passion she had for him. Her mind and soul sank deeper into the kiss, and she thought she would fall into an unconscious abyss from the force. Her fingers clutched his shoulders for support, and her heart was ready to explode out of her chest with an abnormally fast pounding.

He clamped one hand in her hair, coaxing her further into him. Her mouth willingly opened even more to allow both of them better access. Their tongues and hearts danced with each other, heightening to a level of intensity that she'd never experienced before, including with him, for she'd never needed him as she needed him now. She'd missed him, and she wanted him to know just how much.

She pushed him toward the couch in the keeping room. He lifted his mouth briefly from their kiss and a half grin inched up his jaw.

"Are you in control, Yaz?" he breathed against her lips.

"Shhh, be quiet." She shoved him back on the couch and straddled him, claiming his lips once more before he said anything else.

But he stopped their kiss and lowered his gaze to the open part of her blouse. His finger traveled down her face to her neck. Yasmine fought to push down the shudder that tore through her as his eyes held hers in a knowing, sensual connection. Cannon's fingers explored her neck, circling around to the spot. *His spot.* Yes! She'd longed for his touch there, and her pulse sped up as he caressed it while his gaze stayed on her in a serious expression. He unbuttoned her blouse, placing kisses down her skin as he unfastened each button. He eased the blouse off her, which she happily threw across the kitchen.

Her breathing became unsteady as he lowered his lips to her exposed collarbone and journeyed a scorching path in between her breasts. His fingers still massaged the back of her neck, inching up into her hair, causing her to finally exhale after having been without him for so long. He unhooked the front snap on her bra to expose her breasts. Her eyes fluttered shut as she absorbed the heat of Cannon's mouth on her skin. She'd dreamed of remembering to know once again what it was like to be intimate with the only man she truly loved. Cannon had been the one to make her feel alive. Exquisite. Loved. Beautiful. Yasmine knew she said she wanted to take it slow with him this time around, but the aching she had for him, she could no longer control herself in his presence. The way his skilled tongue explored her breasts teasing, sucking, nibbling on her pebbled nipples, sent trembling sensations from her head all the way down to her pink toenails. She must've been insane if she thought she was actually going to wait three months to make love to him. Hell, she'd waited twelve years. That was definitely torture long enough.

"You're so damn beautiful, Angel face," he said in a rough, sexy voice that sent heat to escalate through her veins. "I'm going to show you just how much I've missed you for the rest of the night. Maybe some of tomorrow morning as well."

He claimed her lips once more in a raging, commanding kiss, taking the breath of out her lungs. She lifted his sweater over his head and tossed it on the floor with her blouse. The scent of him mixed with his soap from his recent shower, whiffed into her nose, and she wanted him to take her right now on the couch. She pressed herself against his rock bare chest, feeling the intensity of his heartbeat against her body, and kissed his lips with the pent up urgency that had been buried in her for so long. His hands clenched her butt cheeks as he lifted her off of the couch and flipped her onto her back, his lips never leaving hers. He laid on top of her, moving his hands over her body and down to the belt of her jeans. His lips broke off from hers, which caused a pleading moan to escape from her lips. However, when his tongue glided down her neck, she was thankful that his lips were still on her.

With her belt out of the way, he unbuttoned and unzipped her jeans, pulling them down with one hand as he moved his lips and other hand down to her breasts. She wiggled free of the jeans followed by her socks. His heated gaze raked over her naked body, and she knew that intense familiar stare. There wouldn't be much foreplay. He wanted her right then.

He slid his body on top of hers and lowered his lips to hers once more, but this time it was a slow, sensual pace. He dug his hands into her hair as she wrapped her legs around his trim waist. Her hands traced his clean shaven face, moving up to his hair while their sensual kiss turned up a few notches with every moan from her. They continued swallowing each other's moans while trying to press their bodies as close as possible to each other. The heat radiating from his body mixed with her own heat, made her feel as if she was in a kiln, and she knew from experience with him, it was only going to get hotter. If the smoke detectors in the kitchen went off, she wouldn't be surprised.

He continued the assault on her lips, deepening the kiss as his hand moved in between them and down to her aching center that was already wet with passion for him. With one finger, he circled around the little rose bud, and she let out a cry of ecstasy. Cannon knew just the right way to touch and kiss every inch of her, and she shook with the pleasure of knowing that her neglected body would finally be satisfied again by the one man that made her his years ago. No one since him knew what the hell they were doing. Cannon had always focused on her enjoyment with every kiss and touch. He'd always made her feel as if she was the only one in his life. As if she was the only woman he'd ever made love to.

As his finger twirled around her climatic spot, the need of wanting him to go even lower surged through her. She ran her fingers down his smooth back, erupting a low moan from him. She wasn't the only one that remembered turn on spots, and moved her lips from his mouth to the side of his neck up to his ear to nibble and lick it.

"Damn," he whispered. "I know you're trying to …"

She sucked on his ear, lightly squeezing the skin between her teeth. "Trying to what?" she asked slyly as she knew exactly what she was doing.

Instead of answering, he lowered his finger, gliding through the folds of her vagina lips and into the opening of what she craved for.

"Mmmm … yes, that's what I want … for now."

"Goodness … I … know," he stammered out as she slid her tongue down his neck.

"I missed you, Cannon. I want you so bad." She gyrated her hips against the hardness that was protruding through his jeans. Her body trembled as she remembered just how endowed he was.

"And you're going to have me," he said with his lips on hers. "I just want to enjoy you a little more before I take you into the bedroom."

He entered another finger, and a moan she didn't recognize as her own voice echoed throughout the room. Her back arched, and she held onto his neck, unable to restrain the surges shooting through her as he sped up his fingers in an attempt to give her the first of many orgasms that he was going to bestow upon her.

"We can make love right here," she breathlessly said. "I don't care where. I just need to feel you inside of me again." She sounded like a drug addict looking for the next hit, but she didn't care. She had to have him, especially if he kept pumping his fingers—which were becoming slicker with every second—faster.

He kissed the top of her forehead and inched down to her neck.

"I need you in my bed." A guttural groan escaped his throat. "Dreamed about making love to you in my bed. Trust me, I want you so freaking bad."

The bulge in his jeans pressed even more against her, confirming the truth in his words.

More unfamiliar sounds came out of her as she moved her hips against his fingers, feeling every single sensation ravage through her.

"Oh, Cannon ... please ... Yes! Keep ..."

She felt herself falling off of the couch as she tried to hold onto his neck, but she slipped off as he continued to wreak pure blissful havoc on her. He managed to still be on the couch, her legs wrapped around him as he sat on the edge staring down at her with a hungry lust in his eyes.

"Is it good, baby?"

"Yes ... so damn good." Her right leg began to tremble, and he smiled knowingly.

"Are you about to come for me, baby?" His voice was low and hard, and she loved the sound. She loved when he was in the danger zone because that meant he was going to give it to her so good she wouldn't be able to walk straight afterwards. She couldn't believe she'd been deprived from this type of ecstasy for so long. No wonder she was begging this man.

"Goodness ... yes!" She turned her head from side to side, pumping her hips up to him, as both of her legs began to shake with sensations soaring from her womanhood. He moved her legs from around him, and leaving them on the couch, he slid down to the floor. Placing his forehead on hers, his fingers still worked their magic.

"I want to hear you."

She could only nod her head because the explosive vibrations were building up, ready to burst.

"Awwww ... yes ... baby ..." She managed to stumble out with some other words she didn't comprehend, but who cared? She needed to get out the electric shock waves that tore through every cell in her body. She held onto his neck for dear life for she was floating. The floor was no longer underneath her—just complete air surrounded her.

"I ... whhhhat ... I mean ... wherrrre?" She tried to talk, but for some reason the English vocabulary had left her and was replaced by gibberish.

He chuckled. "Are you tongue tied?"

She simply nodded. Burying her head in his chest, she closed her eyes. As her breathing returned to almost normal, she felt herself once again floating on air. She opened eyes and realized Cannon was carrying her upstairs.

"Where are we going?"

"Heaven."

Cannon laid Yasmine down on the bed, kissing her softly, but she pulled him deeper into her mouth with erotic passionate kisses and dragged his body on top of hers. She hastily fumbled with the button and zipper on his jeans. He wasn't surprised with her actions. He knew after the episode downstairs, she wouldn't be able to contain herself and would want him right then and there.

He stood and pulled down his pants along with his boxers, his erection pointing toward her, hard as a flag pole. She sat up on her knees and kissed the middle of his chest, as he caressed her hair. She made little circles with her warm tongue around his nipples and ran a hand down to his other cannon as she always called it.

His original mission was to take it slow, but her tongue was changing his mind. He pushed her back onto the bed and pinned her hands to the mattress with one of his hands as the other one fumbled under the pillow. He pulled out a condom pack and tossed it on the other side of her before taking possession of her lips in an aggressive manner. She wrapped her legs around his waist and thrust her hips up to him.

"Is that a hint?" he asked with his lips on hers.

She managed to wiggle out one of her hands away from his and reached out to grab the condom.

"Yes," she answered in a breathless whisper as she opened the packet and handed it to him. He sat up and secured the protection. He raised her legs around his waist as her body shook with anticipation.

He kissed her lips, gliding his tongue across the bottom one before sinking it into her mouth once more, drawing impatient moans from her. His hands raked down the side of her body and rested on her hips. In one swift move, he was halfway nestled inside of her and an exhaling moan escaped her lips. She wiggled her hips as he slid the rest of the way in. A single tear fell down her cheek, and he kissed her softly as an amazing smile spread across her face.

"I've hated being without you," she said.

"I know, baby. Me too."

He began to move at a slow tempo so she could accommodate his size again. Her muscles were tightening around him with every stroke, and the deeper he indulged, the tighter her walls became. She met his rhythm, reaching her hips up to meet and sink him down into her. He watched her face evolve into beautiful expressions of ecstasy, and her moans escalated throughout the room, all of which caused him to speed up his pace.

"I was wrong earlier," he said in her ear. "I'm not going to show you all night how much I've missed you. I'm going to show you for the rest of my life because that's how long it will take."

"Promise?"

"Goodness, yes!" His body began to buckle and become undone with every stroke and moan from her. He wanted their first time after so long to be longer, but neither could contain their need for each other as they both climaxed at the same time, their cries of love for each other filling the room.

Hours later they lay intertwined on the top of the sheets after a few more rounds of lovemaking. He looked down and smiled as Yasmine rested peacefully on his chest. He ran his hand through her short hair, which thanks to all of their sweating, was half straight and half curly. She let out a soft moan, causing his semi-awake erection to awaken a little more. He pulled her closer into his embrace and smiled as he remembered she was sleeping in his shirt, which he had always found quite sexy. The top two buttons were undone, and the shirt had risen up around her stomach exposing her plump, bare bottom. She scooted closer to him, and he realized she may be cold since the covers were around her knees. He reluctantly pulled the cover up to her forearms, and she softly moaned and stirred in his arms.

"You're awake?" she asked.

"Hey, sleepy head."

"Mmmm…what time is it?"

"It's a little after midnight."

"You know we aren't done right?"

"You can go again?" He sat up with his newfound energy.

She chuckled. "Perhaps, but I was referring to the wedding favors. There's about five pounds of bird seed waiting to be wrapped in tulle."

He smacked his lips together and popped her butt. "We'll get to that later. But tell me something. I'm a little curious to know the last time you … um … had sex."

She sat up and thumped his forehead and wrinkled her nose in a cute smile. "Why are you being so nosey, Dr. Nosey?"

"Okay, I don't really want to know, but well you were quite tight the first time and the more I went in, the tighter. It was like unexplored territory, which is a good thing …" he said, grinning.

She straddled him, shaking her head and laughing. "Get that goofy, smug grin off of your face. Let's just say not only are you the best I've ever had, you're also the …" her voice trailed off as she planted a kiss on his mouth.

He slapped her butt cheeks and gave her a cocky smile. "Figures."

She reached under the pillow and pulled out three more condom packs. "And why were all these condoms under your pillow?" She plopped them down on his chest and sat up with her arms crossed, raising a teasing eyebrow.

"Because, woman," he said, flipping her over on her back, bringing out a laughing gasp from her, "I placed them there after my shower. You came in my house fine as Argentine wine in those sexy white skinny jeans. Besides, it was written all over your face when I opened the door."

She pinched him playfully on the arm. "You tricked me. Opening the door practically naked. I've been hot and bothered all night." She ran her hand down to his fully aroused erection and gave it a strong stroke. "Looks like someone is ready to go again."

"Of course. I'm the best you've ever had."

CHAPTER NINE

"Wow. This is your parents' new home?" Yasmine asked as they pulled up into the long, winding driveway of a two story colonial-styled brick home with tall white columns on the front porch. The Arrington's were having a family cookout since it was a beautiful spring day, and their parents had just returned from a two-week European vacation and wanted to see their children.

"It's gorgeous," Yasmine continued as she stared in complete awe. "The landscaping is beautiful."

"Mother did a lot of the planting of the flowers and shrubs along with a horticulturist at the botanical gardens," Cannon said. "You know my mom doesn't mind getting dirty."

"I remember. Can't wait to see her."

"She can't wait to see you, either."

Moments later they walked into the house and could see straight through the two-story foyer to the veranda. Justin was at the grill in the outdoor kitchen, along with Shelbi. They were cooking all of the meats. Everyone else was asked to bring a side dish.

"Let's see where Shelbi wants the pasta salad."

"Okay," Yasmine answered. She was a little nervous. She hadn't seen the Arrington family in years except for Shelbi. She'd always gotten along with them, but she didn't want anyone to jump to the conclusion that her and Cannon were officially back together. They were still taking things one day at a time.

"Is that my girl?" a woman's voice asked.

Yasmine felt a pinch on her arm and turned around to see Dr. Darla Arrington, Cannon's mother. She didn't seem to have aged one bit, except her reddish-brown natural curls that Raven had inherited were almost all gray. She still had the glowing, smooth cocoa skin that Bria and Sean also had and the charming, witty smile that Shelbi and Cannon possessed.

Yasmine had been very close to his mother and had kept in contact for a few years after the breakup, but after a while it became hard because Dr. Darla would always mention his name, and Yasmine didn't want to hear about anything he was doing.

"Hello, Dr. Darla." The ladies hugged. "It's so good to see you."

"Missed you, but I'm so glad you and Cannon are back together." Dr. Darla squeezed her tight and kissed her cheek. "My son was a wreck over you for years. Now maybe he'll give me some grandbabies."

Cannon glanced at Yasmine. "We're taking things one day at a time; however, I'm never letting her get away from me again."

Dr. Darla took Yasmine's hand and led her outside. "When it's meant to be, it's meant to be." She smiled and squeezed Yasmine's fingers.

Moments later, Yasmine found herself at a table by the pool with Shelbi and Dr. Darla. Cannon was the designated bartender and was in the outdoor bar area making strawberry rum daiquiris for the ladies.

"So glad you decided to have a cookout, Mother," Shelbi said. "It's finally a warm day in Memphis."

"It's almost May, so expect plenty more." Dr. Darla looked toward the veranda. "And as long as my children cook and I supply the house, you can come every weekend. Oh, there's Bria and Rasheed, but what's that dish she's holding?"

Shelbi turned around in her chair to investigate, and then back to face her mother with a look of terror on her face. "Mother, I promise I told her to bring the paper goods, no food."

"Bria," Dr. Darla called out with a wave. "What did you bring, sweetheart?"

Everyone stopped what they were doing and looked in Bria's direction. Justin had tongs midair with a rib in it, Cannon stopped the blender, and Dr. Darla's hand was over her heart.

"Paper goods and a salad," Bria answered, setting everything on the food table under the veranda.

"A ... salad?" Shelbi asked nervously. "What kind of salad?"

"Relax people," Rasheed stated. "She didn't cook anything. It's just spinach leaves, feta cheese, pecans, and strawberries with a raspberry vinaigrette dressing. The chef helped."

Everyone breathed a sigh of relief and went back to what they were doing.

"She can't cook that well," Shelbi whispered to Yasmine as Bria walked over to the table. Bria was just as Yasmine remembered. Long, dark brown hair, a clear cocoa complexion and besides the baby bump protruding from her like a basketball, she was still a bean pole.

Bria pulled Shelbi's ponytail. "I heard you," she said laughing, and gave Yasmine a hug. "Good to see you again. It's about time you and my brother reconnected."

"Good to see you, too. Congrats on the marriage and the baby." Yasmine wanted to rub Bria's cute baby bump, but she knew some women didn't care for that. "Your salad sounds delish. I make a similar one with blueberries and almonds."

Bria kissed her mother's forehead and sat across from her. "It's one of things I've been craving lately, so that's why I brought it. Next week, it will be something else. Where's Raven and Sean?"

Cannon came over with a pitcher of the daiquiri and three red plastic cups. "I'll be back with a virgin one for you, sis." He kissed Bria's forehead before walking away.

Dr. Darla poured the frozen mixture as she answered Bria's question. "Raven is at the hospital. One of her patients is having an emergency C-section but will come later, and Sean is running late."

Moments later, Sherika and Doug arrived. Yasmine was glad to see her best friend. Even though they talked, texted, Skyped, and emailed almost every day, she hadn't seen her in person since Thanksgiving. After they ate, the two friends decided to take a walk in the gardens in the backyard. The tulips were in bloom and the Knock Out roses were beginning to bloom beautifully. Dr. Darla's garden reminded Yasmine of the botanicals gardens with the walking trails, flower beds that actually had miniature signs with the names of the plants, and different colored solar lights along the border.

"So how was the meeting with the coordinator?" Yasmine asked.

"It went well," Sherika said, sitting on the bench and taking a sip of the strawberry margarita Cannon made for her. "You know, I think Cannon was a bartender in his other life. This is good," she said as a deep smile crossed her toffee face, showcasing her cute dimples.

"I know." Yasmine laughed. "He's a keeper. So is there anything else you need us to do?"

"Everything is pretty much done thanks to you and Cannon. Now I have to wait six more weeks, and I'll be Mrs. Douglas Winters." She smiled and let out a sigh.

"I'm so excited for you and Doug. But wait … you're moving to Spain. I'll miss you," Yasmine said with a slight pout. In all of the excitement of planning the wedding and being back with Cannon, it just hit her that her best friend was moving out of the country.

"I'll miss you, too. But we'll come to the states to visit, and you and Cannon can come to Spain."

"Ha. I don't know about me and Cannon coming at the same time, but I'll definitely be there."

"What do you mean by that? You're back together or at least working on it."

"I'm moving back to Atlanta after your wedding. I'm teaching two classes in the summer session that starts in July. I'm enjoying my time with Cannon right now, but I don't know what's going to happen down the road, so that's why we're just taking it day by day and getting to know each other again."

"And how's that going?"

"Perfect. I don't want to go back to Atlanta, but I don't want to rush anything either."

"Has he said anything about you leaving?"

"No, not really. He got kind of quiet when I told him I had classes this summer and then asked me how I liked teaching college students."

"Well, would you move back to Memphis if he asked?

"In a heartbeat."

"Good. And who knows, Doug and I may be flying back to the states for your wedding sooner than you coming to see us."

"After planning your wedding, I think I'd rather elope." Yasmine laughed as she got off of the bench, and they made their way back to the pool and veranda area.

When they walked up, Yasmine spotted Cannon leaning on one of the brick columns on the veranda drinking a beer and talking to Sean and Doug.

Cannon flashed his charming smile as she approached and Yasmine's heart melted. The thought of moving back to Atlanta weighed heavy on her mind. The idea of being away from him again was too much to bear. Since they'd made love a few weeks ago, she'd spent every night with him, wrapped liked a cocoon in his arms. She loved his breathing on her neck as he slept, or wearing his dress shirts after him just to feel his warmth and smell his scent on her. She remembered after they broke up, she found one of his shirts hanging in her closet that she didn't notice during her closet clean out when she threw all of his clothes at him. At first she was going to throw the shirt away, but instead decided to keep it. Occasionally during the years when she was in a melancholy state of missing him, she'd pull it out and sleep in it.

After the family cookout, they headed back to Cannon's home. It was wonderful seeing his family again except for his father. He was at a fundraiser with one of the organizations he belonged to.

"Why are you so quiet, Yaz?"

"No reason. Just enjoying the night air."

Cannon had driven Yasmine's car and had the convertible top down. Of course she was lying. Something Sherika said was nagging her. In six weeks was the wedding. Soon after that Yasmine was moving back to Atlanta. Memphis was only a seven hour drive, but they both had busy schedules. Would they only see each other on the holidays? Maybe once a month on the weekends? Yasmine had never been in a long distance relationship before, and she didn't want to experiment with Cannon. He was the type of man she needed to be with and see if not every day but at least have the convenience of it if necessary. She loved sleeping next to him. She loved cooking for him. She loved just being with him.

"This reminds me of the beach air. I haven't been to a beach in ages." Yasmine pushed the button on the side of the seat to let it go all the way down so she could look up at the stars. Cannon's parents lived in Germantown, which was almost a forty-five minute drive from his home in midtown Memphis.

"Really? You want to go?"

"Sure. When?"

"I can move some patients around on my schedule during the next week or so. My family owns a beach house on Hamilton Beach Island."

"In Florida?"

"Yep. My father went to Morehouse with Caesar Hamilton the third. He owns the island and pretty much everything on it. His three sons run everything. I'm cool with Caesar the fourth. He owns a night club and one of the golf resorts. My parents have a condo at the resort, but I'd prefer to stay at the beach house. It's more secluded."

Yasmine sat up and scooted toward Cannon, resting her head on his shoulder. He took his hand off of the gear shift and placed it on her thigh.

"I would love to go."

"Cool. I'll have the receptionist rearrange my schedule, so maybe we can leave next Saturday and stay for about five days. I'll call my mom and make sure no one is using the house. Plus, she arranges a cleaning crew to come before anyone goes to stay. Also, I'll hire a private chef and a housekeeper while we're there so we don't have to do anything except relax."

"Cannon, you don't have to do all of that."

He patted her thigh before moving his hand to shift a gear. "I want to. You deserve it."

"Thank you."

"I meant to ask you. How did you learn how to drive a stick shift? I remember trying to teach you how to drive my Mustang, and you almost ruined the clutch."

"A friend of mine taught me a few years ago. I really wanted this car, and it was cheaper to get a manual as opposed to an automatic."

"What's her name?"

"What makes you think it was a female?" She looked up at him and noticed his jawline was tight. "His name is Demond. He lives in Atlanta. He moved with me when I left New York."

"Is he an ex boyfriend or something?"

"Or something." She shrugged, laughing in her head. *Was he really acting jealous?*

"What the hell does that mean?" he demanded rather harshly.

"Don't worry about it. Let's just say I mastered a stick shift even more now that I'm an older and more experienced driver."

Cannon put both hands tightly on the steering wheel. His jaw was clenched and his right eye was twitching. She knew all of his facial expressions, mannerisms, and body language and inside he was boiling. *Now, I could either tell him the truth that Demond is my gay best friend or I could continue to lie and see his face crack. I think I want him to crack. Definitely crack.*

"You know, Demond is a very nice guy." She stifled a giggle. "He may be coming down in a few weeks to visit. He says he misses me so much. We were together all the time. You should meet him."

"Now why would I want to meet a man that you've been with?"

"Who said I've been with him?"

"He moved down with you from New York. Men just don't pack up and move to another city unless they're serious."

Yasmine could no longer contain her laughter and laughed out loud.

"What's so damn funny?"

"You, Dr. Nosey. You know doggone well you don't want to know about my dating past. However, Demond and I have never dated. We're just great friends. Sherika and I met him in New York, and it was love at first sight."

"So he's Sherika's ex?"

"No. Trust me. He does not want me or Sherika."

"I wouldn't say that. You two are beautiful women. I'm sure if given the chance he would've jumped at it."

"And his life partner would've had a fit."

"Life partner?" Cannon turned his head toward her with a confused expression.

"Yes, his life partner, Charles. That's why Demond moved to Atlanta."

He chuckled. "Woman, never do that again. About to give me a heart attack. I know you had a dating life after me and you're right, I really don't want to know. Not jealous or anything. It's just a man thing, babe."

Leaning over, she kissed him on his cheek. "You're the only one that has truly ever made me happy, and I'm going to show you as soon as we get home." She trailed her tongue down his neck and sucked gently on the spot that always sent him over the edge before sitting back in her seat.

"Why did you stop?" He tugged the hem on her sundress up, exposing her thighs, and settled his hand in between them.

"That was just a taste. Don't worry, you'll get plenty more when we get home."

Home? She really needed to stop saying that. Soon she'd be home in Atlanta, but now she didn't want to go back.

Cannon turned into his driveway moments later. Pushing the garage door opener, he pulled into the garage. "You know you were wrong for lying to me." His sexy, dangerous tone created a heat between her legs that sped through her veins.

"I didn't lie. You insinuated. What are you going to do? Take me over your knee and spank me?" she asked, running her hand up his thigh and settling on the hard bulge in his pants.

"Get in the house," he demanded, unclicking his seatbelt and then hers. "You've been a naughty girl."

Hours later, they lay intertwined together on the damp comforter on the kitchen floor. She'd gone to the kitchen earlier wrapped in the comforter after two rounds of lovemaking to grab two bottled waters when Cannon came up behind her, yanked the comforter off, and bent her over one of the barstools. Driving her completely insane, he kissed the back of her neck and gave her long yet gentle strokes that caused amorous sounds to escape from her. How they ended up on the floor she had no recollection. After the orgasm slammed through her body, she blacked out for a moment from the impact before flipping him on his back and riding him until he shook so hard underneath her she thought surely the neighbors would think there was an actual earthquake in Memphis.

Yasmine ran her finger along his chest and kissed his scar before settling her head over his heart. Their legs were looped together like a pretzel as they lay side by side. He was definitely fast asleep. She wanted to wake him so they could go back to the bedroom, but he seemed at peace with his head nuzzled on hers, and his soft snores filled the room. Normally, snoring would disturb her, but from him it was a tranquil sound that she didn't mind. There was a cool breeze emerging from the vents of the air conditioner, blowing over them and adding to the at peace feeling that loomed around her.

She wasn't sure what was going to happen with their relationship when she returned to Atlanta, but for now she was happy to be in his embrace again.

CHAPTER TEN

Yasmine placed the last of her beach necessities in her tote bag and tossed it on the bed. It was the second day of their getaway at the Arrington family beach home on Hamilton Island. They'd flown in late last night from Atlanta, after spending a day at Yasmine's home because she hadn't seen it since January.

They spent the morning touring the island. When they'd returned, they made love and afterwards Cannon left her to nap and do some paperwork for an upcoming project he was working on for Doctors Unlimited.

Walking out onto the balcony of the master suite, she stared out at the sparkling blue water of the ocean. There were families and couples out on the beach either under their umbrellas, or some ladies stretched out on their stomach with their bikini tops off to obtain a tan. She couldn't wait to walk along the beach, to feel the snow white sand between her toes and take in the beautiful blue water of the Gulf of Mexico. She remembered visiting Pensacola Beach often as a child with her parents. She would build sandcastles with her dad, and he would take her out into the water to ride the waves while her mother sat on the beach screaming out to her husband, "Don't take my baby out so far." Of course, her dad would ignore her, and they'd have a play argument when he returned.

Yasmine missed those fun times with her father. Life with him had been too short. She wished he was still alive so she could listen to his jokes that only she found funny, or give her piggy back rides every time she asked for a pony. He never got to see her win her first chess tournament, he wasn't there on her first date to threaten the boy taking her out, he wasn't there to see her graduate from college, and if she ever got married, he wouldn't be able to walk her down the aisle. She smiled and wiped away a tear. He would've loved Cannon—well, maybe not after their break up—but the two men had a lot in common such as love of their careers, love of family, and helping those less fortunate. Whenever she complained about something frivolous, her father would drive her to some of the most poverty stricken neighborhoods in Memphis and show her children who didn't have as much as she did. He would tell her they didn't know where their next meal was coming from and didn't have the same educational opportunities as she did. She contributes those moments to why she was an educator. There were times when teaching her college classes that she sometimes missed teaching young children who needed her more than her young adult students.

Yasmine noticed Cannon walk out onto the patio. He slipped his T-shirt over his head, exposing his smooth chest and six-pack of abs. His butterscotch skin was gorgeous as the sun glistened on his hard muscles. He jumped off of the diving board into the deep end of the pool and swam effortlessly to the other side. Lifting his head up to take a breath, he up-righted himself and waded in the water when he saw her. Their eyes locked. His gaze perused over her body and that's when she remembered she was wearing a black string bikini. A wicked smile crossed his face.

"Did you have a nice nap, Yaz?" he asked with a glimmer in his eyes.

"Yes. I needed my rest. Someone keeps putting me to sleep."

"Just doing my job." He pretended to brush fake dust off of his shoulder.

She laughed. "Well, you should receive the Employee of the Year award."

"You're coming to join me in the pool?" He lifted himself out of the water and stood on the cement. Water glided down his body, and his blue swim trunks clung to his thighs, exposing a slight erection. "It's nice and warm."

"No ..." she stammered at his fine physique. "I'm going down to the beach to finish reading my book. You know the one I was going to read earlier before someone scooped me up and tossed me on the bed?"

"Well ... if you change your mind, I'll be here." He winked and jumped back into the water.

Five minutes later, she placed her tote bag on the lounge chair, threw off her sarong, and sat on the edge of the pool while Cannon swam a few laps not noticing she was there. She loved the water, but because she didn't know how to swim, she preferred lounging by the pool.

When Cannon realized she was sitting there, he smiled and waved from the other side.

"I see you changed your mind?"

"Yep. I'll go out to the beach in a little bit. I wanted to watch you swim." She didn't even know why she was going to go the beach when she wanted to spend every single possible moment with him. The thought of going back to Atlanta soon made her sad. She wished she didn't have the two classes to teach during the summer session, but she'd already signed her contract.

He went under the water in a straight target to her. When he surfaced, he lifted up between her legs, placing them on his shoulders.

"Hey you." He leaned in for a kiss.

"Don't pull me into this water," she said, laughing and trying to move her legs back, but he wrapped his arms around them, holding them firmly on his shoulders

A sexy grin crossed his face. "I thought you liked your legs on my shoulders."

"I do on land, not in the water. You know I can't swim."

"Still can't swim, huh? None of your ex boyfriends taught you how?"

"Very funny." She scooted back on the cement, and he let go.

"Slide into the water with me."

"I'm good."

"Don't you trust me?"

"Yes," she said with a wide smile. She knew where this conversation was going to end up just by the lazy, seductive tone of his words.

"Leave your shades on the side and come in. I know you're not wearing that sexy bikini just to walk around in, even though I do appreciate it."

She laid her shades on the concrete and slid into the warm water with her back against the wall of the pool. They were in five feet so her feet did touch the bottom, but at five foot six, she was reluctant to leave her spot. She loved the water, but she'd never been thrilled with being under it after her swim coach tossed her into the deep end when she was only seven. It terrified her because she wasn't expecting to be thrown in, and she refused to go back to the lessons.

"Go out with me to the middle." His arms came around her waist, and he moved her body a few inches away from the wall. "I got you."

She could feel his penis floating around her stomach through his trunks. *How can this man possibly be hard in the water? Oh wait. I'm wearing a string bikini.*

"Just hold onto me." He kissed her forehead. "I'm not going to let you go." He lifted her legs around his torso, and she held onto his neck, probably tighter than necessary.

"Are you okay, Angel face?"

"Yes." And she was because he was holding her, and she trusted him with all of her heart.

"I'm not going to take you to the deep end … well at least not in the water." He winked and kissed her softly on the lips. "Just going to carry you out to the middle, and when you feel comfortable, lift your legs back behind you."

"I'd rather they stay wrapped around you." She laughed nervously as she tightened her grip on him.

He chuckled as he walked backwards with her slowly out to the middle, keeping his gaze on her. "You trust me, baby?"

"I'm not too heavy?"

"Ha. You're weightless in the water. But answer my question."

"Yes, I trust you."

"Good. Lift your legs. I got you."

She loosened her grip around his torso, but tightened her arms around his neck. Slowly, she lifted her legs out behind her as straight as possible, and he continued wading backwards.

"Move your legs under the water … you know, as if you're swimming." He gave her an encouraging smile, and she began to move her legs as instructed.

"You're a very good swim teacher. You've done this before?" she asked, thinking how many other women had he done this with. Besides golf, swimming was his other favorite sport, which was why his house was located in a golf community, and he had an indoor pool so he could swim anytime he wanted to.

"Nope. Only you, my dear." He turned his back toward the deep end.

"Just checking."

"You want to go further?" he asked, releasing her hands from around his neck and holding her arms stretched out from him.

She sighed. So far she was comfortable, but now she wasn't so sure. She needed baby steps. "How many feet is further?" she asked with a croak in her throat.

"Its six feet deep."

"Um ... hello. I'm only five foot six." She refused to panic, but she wasn't exactly thrilled either.

"I'm six foot one."

"Barely. How about we go toward the three feet part instead?" She started to pull his arms.

"How about you trust me," he answered sincerely.

"Cannon ..."

"Trust me, Angel face. I'm *not* going to let you go."

She took a deep breath. "All right. I trust you."

He began to wade backwards with her paddling her legs for dear life. When they made it to the other side, he turned her so that her body was against the wall of the pool. Wrapping her legs around him again, she held onto his neck. He placed his arms over her shoulders as he held onto the side of the pool.

"Are you okay?" he asked.

"Yes. It wasn't as bad as I thought it would be, but can we get out now?"

"Sure, but you do realize that I wasn't going to let you go?" he asked in a serious tone.

"Of course, baby."

"Good, because I love you, Yasmine, and I'm never letting you go again."

Happy tears welled in her eyes. "I love you, too, Cannon. Always have."

An hour later, she rested her head on his bare chest, drawing circles around his scar and breathing in his fresh scent. They'd made love and then took a shower together to wash off the chlorine.

"Yasmine?"

"Yes?"

"What are we going to do about the long distance? I know you have to go back to Atlanta but ..."

"I guess we'll be putting more miles on our cars and earning frequent flier miles."

"Humph. You just came back into my life, and now I can't even see you like I need to."

"Not true. My schedule is a lot more flexible than yours. I'm an adjunct professor. I don't have classes every day. Heck, I don't even have my own office. I have to share with another adjunct."

"What's your class schedule like during the fall?" He sat up, placing his back on the headboard, taking her with him.

"I don't know at the moment. The two classes I teach for the summer session are both on Mondays and Wednesdays for eight weeks."

He sighed. "So you can fly out to Memphis every Wednesday night and fly back on Sundays?"

"Most of the time. I have other responsibilities, but they fall more so during the school year. I teach a lot of workshops for the different school systems. That's how I make my bread and butter."

He kissed the top of her forehead. "I'll pay for your plane tickets, and I'll come to Atlanta as well. We'll make it work. I'm not losing you again."

She looked up at him. "And I'm not going anywhere."

"Even if I grow another head and a third eye on my chest?" he joked.

"Especially then. That means two handsome faces to look at and kiss on."

"What about the third eye on my chest?"

"Okay … that may be a deal breaker." She laughed as he flipped her over and his lips came crushing down on hers. He parted her legs and in one stroke was buried completely inside of her. *Okay, so maybe I'll think about the third eye …*

On their last night on the island after they ate the delicious lobster dinner the chef had prepared, they relaxed in the hot tub staring up at the stars and sipping on champagne. Cannon had turned off the outside lights and lit candles all around the hot tub. It created a romantic ambience when she walked outside completely shocked by his surprise. He had champagne cooling and Duke Ellington strummed through the speakers that looked like rocks in the landscape.

It was simply amazing, and she didn't want their time on the beach getaway to end. After planning the wedding for their friends, they definitely needed the vacation. The only thing left was Doug's bachelor party, which was going to be held in Las Vegas thanks to Rasheed who was letting Cannon use his private jet and connections to stay at a penthouse of one of the casinos. They were to fly out after the rehearsal dinner on Thursday night and come back early Saturday morning.

Yasmine had already begun plans for Sherika's wedding shower/bachelorette party that would last all day on Friday, beginning that morning at the spa with facials, mani/pedis, massages, and a brunch catered by Shelbi. In attendance would be the bridesmaids, Sherika's mother, aunts, and friends. Because Doug and Sherika were moving to Madrid, they didn't want to ship a lot of wedding gifts over. Instead, in lieu of gifts they asked for donations in their name to be donated to their favorite charities. That evening, the real festivities were to begin without Sherika's mother and aunts at the bachelorette party at Yasmine's house. She convinced her mother—which wasn't hard to do—to spend the night at her boyfriend's home.

Yasmine was glad her and Cannon finally had a conversation about their relationship and that it would turn long distance soon. She definitely didn't mind flying to Memphis on most weekends to visit. She'd done that when her mother first started her chemo treatments, but it started to wear on Yasmine mentally and physically, which was why she decided to take the sabbatical. But now this situation was different. She couldn't go to Memphis every single weekend to visit. They both had work commitments and other obligations. What about the times when he would have to go out of the country for Doctors Unlimited? She completely understood those trips, but there could be two to three months where he would be gone at a time. He'd told her a few weeks ago that because of the practice, he didn't like to be out of the country for extended amounts of time. However, he was the CEO of Doctors Unlimited, and he checked on the clinics to ensure everything was running smoothly especially the newer ones.

She sipped her champagne and stared at the handsome man sitting across from her with a sexy expression on his face.

"What are you gazing at?" she asked, gliding over to his side of the hot tub and sitting next to him. He placed his arm around her, and she nuzzled on his shoulder.

"You've been daydreaming for the past five minutes. Whatcha thinking about?"

"Just how relaxing this trip has been. I haven't really just breathed since I found out my mother had breast cancer. I feel like I've been on the move nonstop, and add in planning Sherika's wedding."

"And then me."

"Yes, you, but I'm so happy you're back in my life. I don't even know how I lived it without you."

"I ask that myself every day especially now when I watch you sleep."

"Wait." She sat up and faced him with a wide grin on her face. "When do you do that?"

"Sometimes, I get back up once I've put you to sleep and do some work on my laptop, and I can't help but glance over at your angelic face." He trailed a finger down her cheek, raised her hand, and kissed it gently. "I have to admit, now that you're back in my life, I sleep so much better. I don't know what I'm going to do when you move back to Atlanta this summer."

She sighed, for she didn't know either. "We'll work it out." She squeezed his hand, and he pulled her onto his lap, pressing her forehead against his. "Just take it one step at a time like we've been doing."

He kissed her gently, coiling his tongue around hers in a slow, tender caress releasing erotic moans from her. His hands glided down her back, unhooking her bikini top on the way to her derrière, cupping it and bringing her closer to him. His manhood was nestled in between her thighs, and she wanted to remove his swim trunks and ease herself down on his hardened cannon. The warmth of his lips trailed down to her neck as he removed the bikini top. She leaned back from him, her hair touching the water as he licked and sucked on her neck.

"Are you trying to brand me?" she asked, knowing all that hard sucking would definitely leave a mark.

He laughed quietly. "Already did years ago all over your sexy ass body. Why do you think no other man has ever triggered your erogenous spots?"

"Arrogant ass."

"Thank you." He pulled her up, slid out his trunks, and placed her back on his lap. His hand glided under the water and moved aside her thong bikini bottoms. Lifting her up, he pushed her back down onto his glorious rod inch by inch until he was buried in her to the hilt, hitting her g-spot immediately. Her breathing stifled as she wiggled her hips to get comfortable. Whenever she was on top of him, she always needed to readjust to accommodate his size as a slight pain shot through her gut. His hands clenched her bottom, and he began to move her up and down at a slow pace, eliciting muffled moans from her. She buried her head in the crook of his neck and held onto his shoulders, digging her fingernails into them. This sensual momentum was inflicting passionate waves of heat to crash through her, and she began to speed up their rhythm. Her amorous cries became more fervent in the night air.

He pulled her head out of his neck so that they were face to face. "Oh, so you want it faster?" A sinful smirk inched across his lips.

She leaned over and whispered in his ear making sure her tongue was in it, "I want it every way."

And with that, he began meeting her halfway with hard thrusts, setting her insides on fire. The water around them began to splash out of the hot tub, extinguishing most of the candles, and their erotic moans silenced Ellington's piano masterpiece.

The build up to her climax came as soon as he entered her, and she rocked back into the water as he pulled her to him over and over until she slumped on his chest trying to catch her breath.

"How else do you want it?"

"From ... the back."

"Oh you up for all kinds of challenges tonight?" he said, lifting her off of him. He stood and grabbed a towel from the side, folded it, and placed it back on top of the hot tub.

"It's not a challenge," she said with a slight neck roll. "I can handle what belongs to me."

It was completely dark except for one lone candle, but she could see his sexy smile and his eyebrows go up.

"Oh really? Place your knees up here."

"With pleasure." Once she was in position, she wondered what the hell he was doing back there. She heard the water move behind her, but he still hadn't entered, and she was shuddering with anticipation. And then she felt his hand caress the back of her neck while the other one settled his penis between her butt cheeks, moving it up and down but not entering just yet. *Dammit, he is about to drive me crazy tonight.*

He moved his body over hers and replaced his fingers on her neck with his blazing tongue, releasing an earth-shattering cry. He moved his free hand around to her breasts, kneading and tantalizing them. She banged her palm on the side of the hot tub. How much more stimulation could she take she didn't know. She was so engrossed with his tongue dancing wickedly on the back of her neck, a long surprising gasp escaped from her when he entered with one long thrust. She almost fell over, but he held onto her hips tightly. He pushed her all the way out from him and then all the way back with one long motion over and over. No inch by inch this time. She couldn't contain her passionate moans that became louder with every second. She hoped no one called the police, but the good thing about the Arrington beach house was it was completely secluded. However, as loud as she was, she swore she was breaking the sound barrier.

"You do realize I'm standing still," he whispered in her ear. "I'm only moving you. Let me know when you want me to begin."

"Begin."

Cannon chuckled and kissed the side of her neck as he began to thrust into her, once again sending her almost over the edge of the hot tub, but she knew he wasn't going to let her go.

His thrusts became more powerful as his groans began to match hers. The pain and pleasure he was bestowing upon her seemed to go on forever, and knowing Cannon's stamina, it was, especially when she glanced up and saw that the moon had moved. When she finally felt him about to release he shuddered behind her, slamming into her over and over. His scorching tongue on her neck sent her into a state of oblivion as her orgasms began to overlap each other.

He pulled out of her, and she turned back to see why the hell he stopped. In one swift move, he jumped out of the hot tub and picked her up, carrying her to the outdoor couch under the veranda. Cannon grabbed a condom from under the throw pillow and rolled it on as she almost began to laugh, and he winked at her. He was always prepared for anything no matter what the situation.

He laid down on top of her and raised her legs— that had turned to jelly—around his middle and entered her this time slowly. He moved at a steady pace, which she was grateful for, and he rested his forehead on hers, reaching for her lips in between breathing. She closed her eyes and let the passion and love for him over take her, meeting his unhurried rhythm that was in complete sync with each other. His sweat dripped down on her face. She could taste the saltiness of it, but when she opened her eyes she could make out in the moonlight that it wasn't sweat. The salty taste was falling from his eyes, and she reached up to kiss them. He smiled and kissed her deep as her own emotions welled up.

"Never ... letting ... you go, dammit." He cupped her face in between his hands as tears ran down her cheeks—hers and his. "You hear me?"

"Yes, baby." She placed her hands over his.

Cannon's body quivered against hers, and she could feel the pulsating of his penis inside of her, and she tightened her muscles around it.

"Goodness, Yaz! Shit ... awwww ... baby! Yes ... woooo." He stopped thrusting, and his body shivered as if it was fifty below zero even though it felt more like two hundred degrees, since they were both saturated in hot sweat and tears.

They held onto each other's hands on her face, staring at each other for a while until their breathing returned to normal.

"You look so beautiful with the moonlight shining on you," he whispered.

"I love you."

"I love you, too, Angel face." He kissed her softly. "Can you think about something for me?"

"What's that, Cannon?"

"Moving back to Memphis permanently."

"I can definitely give that some consideration."

CHAPTER ELEVEN

Yasmine sat on Cannon's couch reviewing her syllabus for the regular semester to see how she could reduce it to only eight weeks. She wanted to get her own personal tasks out of the way because Sherika was flying into town tomorrow and getting married four days later. Yasmine knew once her best friend arrived, she wouldn't have any free time. There were last minute fittings, airport pickups, final payments to drop off, and shopping. Sherika had been a nervous wreck the last time they spoke so Yasmine scheduled a massage for just the two of them as soon as Sherika arrived tomorrow morning. Yasmine knew she needed to be with her best friend as much as possible, which meant time away from Cannon, but he had a list of things to do with Doug as well.

Cannon was still at the practice but would be home soon. Dinner was already cooked, and she sighed as she realized she was getting used to their routine.

Her cell phone ringing interrupted her thoughts. She picked it up and saw it was Dean Patrick, who oversaw the English Lit department. Yasmine had left her a voicemail earlier.

"Hello, Dean Patrick."

"Hello, Dr. Dubose. I received your message about the syllabus information."

"Going over it right now."

"Perfect, because I wanted to ask you something. I'm looking at the online enrollment for the class, and it seems that there are more students registering to take the online version. You did an awesome job with the online class last summer, and I wanted to know if you could do it again?"

Yasmine's ears perked up. "Oh. I see. So I'll be teaching the online class in addition to the one on campus?"

"No. I know you're still in Memphis with your mother, so I thought maybe you may only want to do the online one instead. You can teach it right there if you aren't ready to leave your mother yet."

Yasmine's heart stopped, and a wide grin crossed her face. She shook her head in denial. She'd been battling within herself lately because of the fact that she didn't want to leave her mother or Cannon, especially since he'd ask her to consider moving back to Memphis. They hadn't discussed it again, but she knew it was definitely on his mind. She loved living back home again even before Cannon entered the picture and didn't miss the hustle and bustle of her busy life in Atlanta.

"Dean Patrick, I would love to teach the online class this summer. That actually would be perfect."

"Wonderful. I'll email you the new contract and a different version of the syllabus along with some other information. Also, I'm conducting a conference call in a few weeks with everyone about the upcoming school year. I'm making some changes in the department because of budget cuts."

"Am I being cut?" Yasmine always knew that was a possibility considering she was the last adjunct professor hired. Even though the thought of being cut wasn't upsetting her at all now that she was moving back to Memphis eventually.

"I don't want to cut you. I'm thinking about making you one of the full-time professors. The students like you, and you're a very good teacher. I think it's because you started in elementary school first and have a little more patience."

"Wow. Thank you for the compliment and opportunity."

"Well, nothing is set in stone yet. I'm still going over some numbers. Think it over just in case, and I'll contact you when I know something more concrete."

"I look forward to it."

After Yasmine hung up, she went to the kitchen to check on her roast beef in the crock pot and to think about everything Dean Patrick said. Teaching the online class this summer would mean she could stay in Memphis for a little while longer until she decided when she was going to move back permanently. However, the possibility of being a full-time professor was scaring her. Yasmine had always been determined and goal-oriented. When she accomplished one goal, she set another one. But for some reason being a full-time professor had never been one. She enjoyed her freedom of teaching two classes a semester and doing educational consulting on the side. She set her own schedule and wasn't tied down to a nine to five. Full-time professors had more responsibilities on campus with organizations and extracurricular activities. Plus, those extra duties would mean fewer trips to Memphis to visit her mother and Cannon.

The door chimed, and she looked up to see Cannon taking purposeful strides toward her. He picked her up and twirled her around.

"You certainly are in a good mood," she said as he set her on her feet. "Great day at work?"

"It's always a great day at work," he said, loosening his tie and tossing his white coat on a barstool at the island. "And it's an even better day when I come home and you're here." He pulled her close to him and kissed her fully on the lips. "Baby, you taste like strawberries." He kissed her again, licking his tongue on her lips.

"That's because I made you strawberry shortcake." She broke from his embrace and went to the stove to make his plate.

"Okay, you're spoiling me." He encircled his hands around her waist and rested his chin on her shoulder. "I'm going to have a nervous breakdown when you go back to Atlanta after the wedding."

A huge Cheshire cat smile expanded on her face, and she could hardly contain her news. "Well ..."

"Well what, woman?" He playfully spanked her butt. "You want me to have a nervous breakdown so that I end up on Sean's couch spilling my guts to him. He'd love that. He's been trying to analyze me for years."

She giggled.

"What's so funny?"

She turned in his arms and placed her hands around his neck. "You know I mentioned to you earlier that I was revising my syllabus for this upcoming session. So Dean Patrick called and asked me to teach the class online this summer. I did it last summer as well."

He smiled, but then shook his head. "So, before I get too excited, are you doing this in addition to teaching on campus?"

She kissed his cheek. "Nope. Online only. I can do it from anywhere in the world as long as I have Internet access. She's emailing me the new contract."

"So ... you'll stay with me in Memphis this summer?"

"Yes. I do need to go back home for a little bit to take care of some business, but other than that, I'll be here."

"With me?" he whispered, his lips but a centimeter from hers.

"With you and my mother."

He kissed her mouth, cheeks, forehead, and back down to her lips. "Too bad you can't teach the online class in the fall, too. Then you could always be here with me and your mother."

"Oh ... well ... about that." She turned back around and continued fixing their plates.

"More good news?" He kissed the back of her neck.

"Um ... okay you know I can't concentrate when you do that. I don't know if it's good or bad, but when I spoke to Dean Patrick earlier she mentioned the possibility of me being a full-time professor when I return in the fall, but it's not set in stone."

"Oh ... well, that is good. Isn't it?" he asked reluctantly and backed away from her as she carried the plates to the table.

"I don't know. I didn't apply for it. It just happened, and she's not sure yet. I think she wanted to put that bug in my ear so I would know."

He went to the butler's pantry, poured a drink, and sat with it at the table, swirling it around in his glass.

"What do you want to do? I mean, that's an honor. You've worked hard, Dr. Dubose." He smiled, but she could tell it was a fake one. "Would you still do your educational consulting on the side?"

"I haven't thought that far, but I know being full-time I would have other responsibilities that I didn't before, so I'd have to see. I don't even know if I want the position." She shrugged.

"Yasmine, that's an opportunity you don't just shrug at."

"But what about us? I may not be able to come here every weekend, or even every other weekend, plus I'm moving back here eventually."

"Yasmine, I'm not going to stand in your way of an opportunity like this. You sacrificed for me. I would be selfish to not do the same for you. We'll just deal with what happens."

"Okay ... but like I said, it isn't set in stone, and I don't have to take it if it's offered to me."

"Why would you not take it? You're an intelligent woman who has worked hard over the years to obtain your goals."

She simply nodded her head and tried to eat her food, but her appetite was lost.

That night, Yasmine laid in bed wide awake and alone. Cannon was in his home office on a conference call for Doctors Unlimited, which had been taking up some of his time lately. He'd briefly told her one of the newer clinics, that he didn't help set up, was having some funding issues or over-spending in some areas, and he wasn't happy about it at all.

She tried not to think about the conversation earlier with Cannon. She knew he meant well. She just wasn't sure if she actually wanted the position even if it was a choice. She glanced at the clock. It was almost midnight, and she needed to be up early to pick up Sherika from the airport. Doug was flying in later and since he was staying with Cannon, Yasmine was going to stay at her mother's house. She cuddled with Cannon's pillow, inhaling his scent, and tried not to worry about the future. He said he would never let her go again, and she trusted that he wouldn't.

"Damn it!" Cannon slammed his fist on the desk. "What do you mean there's money missing and he's disappeared?" he asked Dr. Armand Phillips, one of the doctors in Ghilaua, a small village in Argentina

"I honestly don't know what's going on Dr. Arrington. All I know is Jessie is gone with all of his belongings and most of the funding in the account. We'll be fine with the supplies that we have now for maybe the next month or so unless something really drastic happens."

Jessie was the director over the medical center that the board hired who Cannon was never thrilled about.

Cannon logged into his Doctors Unlimited account. He had money in a reserves account so that wasn't an issue, but the thought of someone running off with close to one-hundred thousand dollars was pissing him off.

"Okay. I'm going to do some readjusting and get some funds to you after I meet with the board for approval, but first I need to close that account. He may still have the access number. In the meantime, do you think you can run things until I find another director?"

"No problem, Dr. Arrington."

"I'm going to rearrange my schedule and try to come there maybe next month after I meet with the board. I …" He was so mad he really didn't know what to say or do. Everyone involved with Doctors Unlimited had always been hard-working, honest people who wanted to make a difference. He couldn't believe this was happening.

"Thank you, sir. I'll make sure everything runs smoothly. I look forward to finally meeting you," Dr. Phillips said in a chipper tone. "You're the reason why I joined Doctors Unlimited."

"Well, I appreciate that. You came highly recommended. I'll be in touch sometime tomorrow."

Cannon check his planner over the next few months. He was speaking at a medical conference in Vegas the following week and then his calendar was clear until another conference in October. He sighed as he thought about Yasmine's news of being in Memphis this summer, but now he may be in Ghilaua straightening out this mess.

Shit! I told the board I didn't think Jessie was a good candidate.

He unlocked his desk drawer and pulled out a small, black velvet box. He opened it, and smiled at the gold wedding band he was keeping for Doug. He then reached into the drawer and pulled out another small, black velvet box and opened it. He beamed at the three-carat princess cut solitaire engagement ring he bought when he came back from Hamilton Beach. His original plan was to ask Yasmine to marry him before she moved back to Atlanta for the summer session, considering she was going to move back to Memphis, but he didn't want her to move back without them being engaged. But now there was a hole in his plans. Yes he was glad she would be able to stay in Memphis a little longer, but now she may have an opportunity to become a full-time professor in the fall. And he may be away this summer, and his love would be in Memphis. What kind of cruel summer was this?

He placed both ring boxes back in the drawer and locked it. Moments later, he climbed into the bed and pulled Yasmine close to him. She was in a little ball on his side of the bed. He kissed her forehead.

"Are you awake?"

"Yes," she said sleepily.

"Well, I guess today is news day."

"Good or bad?"

"Horrible."

She sat up and stared down at him. "Something wrong with Doctors Unlimited?"

He briefly explained the situation with Jessie, and that he may have to go down there to take care of some business after the medical conference.

"I'm so sorry this has happened, but don't beat yourself up over it. I'm sure you'll find another director of the center soon."

"I'm having an emergency board meeting tomorrow morning via Skype. I want to get everything somewhat planned before the wedding this weekend."

"It will all work out. Have faith." She kissed his cheek before turning over. "Good night."

"Good night." He snuggled behind her and was relieved she didn't lash out at him when he mentioned he may not even be here this summer.

"Girl, I'm so glad you decided to arrange massages for us," Sherika said as the masseuse kneaded her back. "I so needed this. Maybe I won't be as stressed this week."

"Nothing to be stressed over … oh … right there on my shoulder …" Yasmine said as the masseuse massaged her tensed spots. "I went through the check list last night and everything is set. Your wedding coordinator really did a great job."

"No, you and Cannon did a great job. I don't know what Doug and I would've done without you. So, how's that going?"

Yasmine sighed, the pain in her neck returning once more at the thought. She told Sherika about her online class this summer, his possible trip to some village she couldn't pronounce, and the offer for the full-time position which was now a go since Dean Patrick called her that morning while she sat in the airport waiting for Sherika.

"That's awesome about the position. How long do you have to decide?"

"She didn't say. She told me to mull it over."

"What did Cannon say?"

"I haven't told him about this morning's phone call yet. However, last night, he pretty much told me to go for it. I was surprised, considering he's been talking about me moving back to Memphis. Um … if I'm in

Atlanta how am I going to do that? He's definitely not leaving the family practice. We've discussed taking things one day at a time, but I don't know. I just thought …"

"Thought what?"

"Well … I thought he was going to propose since he wants me to move back here, but I guess not if he's telling me to take a full-time professor position."

"Maybe he's just being supportive," Sherika suggested.

"I guess, but I was already contemplating moving back home even before Cannon came back into my life. My mother is getting older, and when she had breast cancer I thought I was going to lose her. She's in remission now, but it could come back. I don't want to think negative, but I have to think logically."

The masseuses asked the ladies to turn over on their backs so they could massage their legs and feet.

"What would you do if you were in my shoes, Sherika?"

"Since you aren't interested in the full-time position, I would just keep my adjunct position and get my things in order to move back to Memphis within the year."

"You are truly my best friend and sister. That's what I was thinking. Plus, the school system here really keeps saying they wish I could stay. Maybe I could continue my consulting work with them."

"Girl, you already got this figured out."

Yasmine laughed. "I guess I do. Now to tell Cannon."

CHAPTER TWELVE

Yasmine sat at the head table next to Cannon, along with Sherika and Doug, at their rehearsal dinner upstairs at Lillian's. It was coming to a close, and the men were heading out soon to the private air field to fly to Las Vegas for the bachelor party. Yasmine had barely seen or spoken to Cannon since the bride and groom arrived in town yesterday. He held her hand under the table, smiling at her in a loving way. She knew she was doing the right thing by moving back to Memphis. She had things to wrap up in Atlanta, like selling her home and a few workshops she was already committed to for the school system. She hadn't told him yet. She wanted to talk to him yesterday, but he was stressed with the Doctors Unlimited situation, and her news could wait. However, she wanted him to know before he boarded the plane that night with the guys.

She leaned over and whispered to him, "Cannon, can we chit chat before you leave?"

His eyebrow raised, and he whispered back, "Sure, and you have on a dress. That's perfect."

She giggled. "Not that kind of chit chatting. I mean a real conversation."

"Oh. Yeah. That too. I'll ask Justin if we can use his office."

A few moments later, they were settled in Justin's office. Cannon sat on the couch and Yasmine stood.

"This wedding is finally here," Cannon said, sounding exhausted already. "Just two more days."

"I know. I'm so happy for them."

"What did you want to talk about? I believe we're leaving in a few."

"Well, did you get everything straightened out for the medical team in Argentina?"

He shook his head. "Yes and no. The board has decided before we hire another director that we're going to go down there and see what's really going on."

"When are you leaving?"

"Sometime after the conference. Maybe the beginning of July. I know you'll be here, so you're welcome to stay at my house while I'm away. I shouldn't be gone more than three weeks top, baby."

"Okay," she smiled, "I'll do that. Besides, I think my mother would like that, too. She likes her space."

"What did you want to tell me?"

"Dean Patrick has officially offered me the full-time position," she said nervously.

"Congratulations, baby. When do you start?"

She was a little taken aback. "Well … I haven't said yes. She just told me to think about it, but it would start in September when the fall semester begins, but I may have to do some things before then."

His cell phone beeped, and he glanced at it. "That's Rasheed asking me where the hell I am. The limo is out front." He jumped off of the couch and hugged her. "I'm very proud and happy for you. I think you should go for it." He kissed her cheek. "Gotta go, baby. I'll text you when we arrive in Vegas."

And then he left. What the hell just happened?

"What the hell did I do?" Cannon asked as he sat next to Doug on the plane.

"Let me get this straight ... you told your woman to go for it, but you really don't mean it?"

Sean leaned over the seat from behind them. "Yes, why is that?"

Cannon sighed and turned to Doug. "Why did you invite him?" he asked somewhat jokingly.

"Because he's your brother, and since Rasheed didn't come, we needed someone who knows where all of the best strip clubs are. But, seriously, what's up? I thought you were going to ask her to marry you?"

"I didn't say I wasn't going to, but at the same time, I think it's a wonderful opportunity for her. Years ago she didn't stop me from going to Brazil. Unfortunately I lost her, but we'll make it work, somehow. I love Yasmine, but I'm not going to stop her from following her dreams, either."

"Okay, so what about the three carat rock you showed me earlier?"

Sean leaned back over the seat. "Damn, bro! Three carats? Is it returnable?"

"I'm not returning anything. I just don't want to hold my girl back."

"Well, it will all work itself out if it's meant to be. I mean, look at me and Sherika. We dated briefly years ago but always remained friends, and now we're getting married in two days, and I couldn't be happier. Then there's you and Yasmine. Mine and my boo's meant to be put you two back together. If I had never gotten that job in New York, I wouldn't have started dating Sherika again, fall in love and now we're getting married. Yasmine just happened to be in Memphis to be with her mom, we decided to get married there and needed the two of you to help plan our wedding. Plus, you confused the dates of your medical conference and almost wouldn't be in the wedding. Now tell me what all of that is?"

"I hear you, man, I hear you. Besides, I promised her I'm never letting her go again and I'm not."

Sean clapped from behind them. "Go get your girl, but after we come back from Vegas."

Cannon stood next to Doug, who wasn't even nervous, but Cannon was. He was anxiously waiting for Yasmine to come down the aisle. He'd only spoken to her briefly yesterday. She was at the spa with the wedding party getting facials and what not. He knew last night was the big bachelorette party at her mother's house, and she was busy make preparations for that. When he called her tone was curt and short with him. He couldn't think what he'd done wrong and figured she was just on the edge because of the wedding.

The bridesmaids were currently being escorted by the groomsmen and then the maid of honor would be coming soon after. Doug turned to him for a second and exhaled with a smile. When Cannon turned his gaze back toward the congregation, there was his Yasmine; a vision of loveliness in a white gown, with three white roses in her hair, and carrying a bouquet of white calla lilies tied in a fuchsia bow. At first, he thought it odd that Sherika wanted all of the bridesmaids to wear white, but now he was glad they did. Yasmine looked every bit of an angel in her white straight dress. His heart skipped a few beats as she walked down the aisle slowly to the pianist playing "Canon in D". When her eyes locked with his, he knew in his heart she was the only one for him, and he wasn't going to let her get away. For a minute, he forgot it wasn't his wedding day when she didn't walk to him but instead stood next to the bridesmaids. He smiled, and she displayed her simply amazing one just for him.

Hours later—after pictures, the greeting line, best man and maid of honor toasts, first dance, bouquet and garter toss, and cake cutting—Cannon hadn't been able to get Yasmine alone yet. His eyes scanned the reception hall, and he finally found her talking to her mom and his mom by the champagne fountain.

"Hello, ladies," he said when he approached. "Can I steal my Yasmine away for a moment?"

"Of course, dear," his mother said. "We'll be right here."

He turned and winked knowingly at both ladies who clapped silently. He scanned the room for a moment before his eyes rested on his father who raised his champagne glass and gave a knowing nod before Cannon walked out the door behind Yasmine.

He led her outside to a small garden that was on the side of the building.

"Finally, a breather," she said, sitting down on a bench under a pergola with ivy vines and pink tea roses.

"I know. It has been a long time getting here, but I think they had a lovely wedding." He sat down next to her on the bench and stretched his feet out.

"Yep," she said in the same curt tone she'd used earlier.

"Yaz, is something wrong?"

"No … why do you say that?" She tried to sound pleasant, but he could still hear the disdain in her voice.

"Because I know you. I know when you're happy, mad, or sad. I know if something is bothering you, and in this case, something is bothering you. So what is it?"

She shook her head. "Nothing."

His father told him a long time ago when a woman says nothing it's definitely something.

"Is it because I'll be in Argentina pretty much the entire time you'll be here this summer?"

"Wait?" She turned her head toward him with an attitude. "You said it was only a few weeks."

"Oh ... yeah about that. I may be there for a few months, but I have a solution for that."

"Cannon ... that's not what's bothering me even though now it kinda is."

"What's bothering you, baby?"

"That stupid job offer that you keep pushing me to take. I thought you wanted to be with me." She stood and walked to the other side of the pergola.

And there was her nothing.

"Wait ... Yasmine, I think you're missing the point. All I said was I thought it was a good opportunity. You've worked hard to achieve your dreams, and I wasn't going to stand in the way of them."

She laughed sarcastically. "I turned it down yesterday."

"You did?" He stepped toward her.

"Yes. I never wanted that type of position. I like my flexible schedule the way it is."

"Then why have you been so terse with me?"

"Because I felt like you didn't want to be with me by pushing me to take it. That's not the type of job you just up and quit within the year because you're moving."

"Wait. Where are you moving in a year?" he asked a little too sternly.

"That's what I wanted to tell you the night of the rehearsal dinner, but you left so abruptly. I want to move back to Memphis to be with you and my mother, the two people I love the most."

He pulled her toward him, picked her up, and twirled her around while she laughed her beautiful infectious laugh. He put her down on the bench and stood in front of her.

"You know, I think a year is good."

"Oh really? Why is that?" she asked with a puzzled expression.

He bent down on one knee in front of her as she gasped, "Oh my goodness!" He pulled out the ring box and showed it to her, but didn't open it.

"A year would be good because then you'll have enough time to plan our wedding, that is if you'll give me the honor of being my wife."

Tears streamed down her face as she kissed him before jumping into his arms and they both fell onto the grass. They laughed and kissed some more before he helped her up.

"I'm assuming that was a yes," he said holding her close.

"Yes, Cannon, I'll marry you."

Pulling back, he opened the ring box.

"It's beautiful."

He slid it on her finger and kissed her hands.

"So I guess we have another wedding to plan?" he asked.

"Cannon, if I plan another wedding, I'll scream."

"You're saying you don't want a wedding?"

"I just want to be with you. I don't care about the wedding."

"Hmm … well, when we were in Vegas, there were a lot of wedding chapels there … maybe we can do that next summer or have a destination wedding?"

"You want to wait that long?"

"Yasmine, if I could I'd take you to Vegas right now and marry you."

"Okay." She pulled his hand toward the building. "Let's go."

He stopped walking. "You're serious?"

"Are you serious?"

"Yes, but you still have the other two classes to teach in the fall, your consulting work, and a house to sell."

"I haven't signed my contract for the fall, only the summer, and while you're in Argentina I'll go back to Atlanta to take care of putting my house on the market."

"No … you're going to Argentina with me. I can't spend that long without my wife."

"I still have the online class during that time."

"Didn't you say you can do the online class anywhere as long as you have the Internet?"

She wrapped her arms around his neck. "Well then, I guess I'm going to Argentina as Mrs. Cannon Arrington."

"You know, you're the only one for me, Yasmine."

"And you're the only one for me, Cannon."

EPILOGUE

Yasmine lounged in the bed with her laptop, reading the midterm exams from her students. She had twenty more to grade before sending them all back at one time. Her and Cannon were finally settled as a married couple of four months. After returning from their one-month stay in Argentina, Yasmine returned to Atlanta for a few weeks to put her house on the market and pack. Most of her belongings had been moved from Atlanta to Memphis into Cannon's home, and she lucked out when her friend Demond decided to buy her house as rental property because of its great location in downtown Decatur.

Dean Patrick was disappointed with Yasmine's decision to not take the position as a full-time professor, but completely understood. She was able to keep her adjunct position and only do two online classes per semester. She was also able to stay on as a part-time consultant with Memphis City Schools.

Yasmine smiled as Cannon entered the bedroom with a tray of kiwi, strawberries, pineapples and non salted crackers.

"Need anything else?" he asked, setting the tray on the bed and sitting on the edge of it.

"Baby, I'm fine." She patted his hand and pushed her laptop aside to sit on his lap.

"I know, but I just want to make sure you have something in your stomach."

She giggled and looked down at her flat stomach, rubbing it tenderly. "What are we going to do with your Daddy?" she asked. "You're so paranoid. It's normal for me to have morning sickness at six weeks. Raven said I'll be fine."

He kissed her forehead and held her tight in his arms. "I know. I just want you to have a comfortable and happy pregnancy."

"And I will with you by my side." She scooted off of him and dragged her laptop back in front of her.

"I guess we'll get in some practice this weekend with RJ while Rasheed and Bria finally get a chance to go out."

"I can't wait. RJ is such a little ham at three months. He reminds me of his Daddy."

Cannon laughed and stood. "That he does." He leaned over and kissed Yasmine on the cheek. "Gotta go to my office for the conference call, Angel face. Is there anything else you need?"

"Nope, thanks to you bringing a mini fridge in here, I'll be fine." She glanced at the refrigerator in the sitting area of their bedroom stocked with all of her favorite healthy snacks.

"All right. The call shouldn't last too long. I have to be at the practice at noon to see patients for the rest of the day. The flu is going around. Which reminds me. You need to come in and have the flu shot done this week."

"Yes, Dr. Arrington, Raven already told me. Anything else?"

"Yes," he leaned over once more and kissed her softly on the lips, and then bent down to kiss her stomach. "I love both of you very much."

Moments later he was in his home office holding the phone in his hand staring at it. He'd just finished the conference call with the board. The clinic in Ghilaua was now without an OBGYN because the replacement one changed her mind. The board did hire another one, but she wouldn't be arriving for another six to eight weeks for personal reasons. Cannon hated for the clinic to go without one for that long, even though Dr. Phillips was a general doctor.

Cannon tapped his finger on his desk and dialed a number.

"Hello?"

"Hey, Raven. I need you to do me a favor…"

~The End~

ABOUT THE AUTHOR

Candace Shaw is the author of fun, flirty and sexy contemporary romance novels. She is a member of Romance Writers of America and Georgia Romance Writers. She is also a member of Alpha Kappa Alpha Sorority, Inc.

When Candace is not writing or researching information for a book, she's reading, window shopping, gardening, listening to music or spending time with her loving husband and their loyal, over-protective weimaraner. She is currently working on her next novel.

Feel free to drop her a line at Candace.Shaw@aol.com or visit her website at http://CandaceShaw.net

BOOKS BY CANDACE SHAW

<u>Arrington Family Series</u>

Cooking Up Love: May 2012
The Game of Seduction: August 2012
Simply Amazing: December 2012 (short story)
Only One for Me: June 2013
Prescription for Desire: TBA
My Kinda Girl: TBA

$10.99

Made in United States
North Haven, CT
15 April 2022

18301627R00125